A GAME OF SENET

PALACE OF THE ORNAMENTS
BOOK FOUR

KYLIE QUILLINAN

First published in Australia in 2024.

ABN 34 112 708 734

kyliequillinan.com

A catalogue record for this book is available from the National Library of Australia.

Ebook ISBN: 9781922852304

Paperback ISBN: 9781922852311

Large print ISBN: 9781922852328

Hardback ISBN: 9781922852335

Audiobook ISBN: 9781922852465

This is a work of fiction. Any similarity between the characters and situations within its pages and places or persons, living or dead, is unintentional and coincidental.

Cover art by 100 Covers

Edited by MS Novak.

This work uses Australian spelling and grammar.

LP21102024

CHAPTER 1

The day I learned Ishtar had probably been murdered was the day my life changed forever. No longer was I the innocent woman sent to Egypt to seal the alliance with Babylon. No longer did I walk the hallways of the Palace of the Ornaments and think this was a safe, if restrictive, place to live. No longer did I look into the faces of the women I passed without wondering how many carried their own secrets. Their own pains. Their own plans.

We said little as Half prepared to leave. He would return to Pharaoh's palace to listen for news of a woman's body being found and confirm whether it was Ishtar. Ahmose had readied two doses of her invisibility potion: one to get him out and another so he could get back in. That was all she had left of the herbs for her special potion, and with the butler, Weren, sniffing around in search of anyone using magic, she couldn't restock. There would be no more opportunities for any of us to get out of the Palace grounds again until it was safe for Ahmose to obtain more of the herb that gave her potion its potency.

In the sitting chamber, I sat with Tall on one side and Ettu on the other. Tall flapped his hands, his worried gaze darting between me and Half, who was talking quietly with Ahmose. I couldn't tell who he was more concerned about. Ettu gave the appearance of being as calm as ever, although the tightness in her body told me she was coiled like a spring.

I wondered whether Ahmose was telling Half about some other magic that might be useful for him while he undertook such a dangerous venture. It had been less than a season since he and Tall fled Pharaoh's palace, with Half mortally injured after being stabbed by a man Tall knew as Userhet. Userhet, who we believed to be a guard, likely still stalked the hallways of Pharaoh's palace and might well try again to kill Half if he saw him. Maybe we should send Tall with him. If it hadn't been for him, Half wouldn't have gotten out last time. Before I could voice my thought, Ettu spoke.

"Will you write to your father?" she asked me. "To tell him…"

Her voice trailed off, but I knew what she didn't want to say. I took a deep breath, testing my words before I replied. Tears welled and I blinked them away. I had already cried so much, I would have thought I didn't have any tears left. Apparently I did.

"Not yet," I said when I thought I could speak through the lump in my throat. "There is still a possibility she will be found safe."

Ettu shot me a look that clearly said I was deluded, although she was kind enough not to say it. We had traced Ishtar's movements on the night she disappeared all the way to Pharaoh. We knew some women were never seen again after meeting with him, and Khaemmalu's friend believed

Pharaoh's captain and his second disposed of their bodies for him. In truth, there was little doubt about her fate, but I couldn't yet let myself accept it.

"I know it's a small possibility," I added, "but I have to believe she might still be alive."

"So where is she then?" Ettu asked gently. "If she is safe, why has she not returned?"

"Maybe she angered Pharaoh and he had her imprisoned," I said. "Maybe he has locked her away to…" Torture her. Abuse her. "For some reason we can't fathom. I don't know. But until someone has seen her body, I can't tell my father. It will break his heart."

Ishtar had always been his favourite, right up until the moment she told Father she was with child. He had already promised a daughter to Pharaoh to seal the alliance with Egypt and it was supposed to be she who went, but he could hardly send Pharaoh a pregnant bride. So he sent me in her place. Never mind I had no wish to leave my home and spend the rest of my life in a land that was as foreign to me as living amongst the stars would be.

But however angry Father was with Ishtar, he was even more incensed when the babe didn't live to be born. He sent her to Egypt anyway to be my maid, as punishment for her failures, both in finding a way to avoid being sent to Pharaoh and then failing to deliver his grandchild. I wondered whether he had another motivation, one he wouldn't have admitted to anyone: that by sending Ishtar, he could ensure at least one of his daughters would bear Pharaoh a child. She was, after all, the beautiful one.

"I don't suppose Pharaoh will write to your father in the meantime," Ettu said.

I studied my hands. The neatly trimmed nails. The well moisturised skin. Such soft, tidy hands. The hands of someone who did nothing useful all day and who had far too many maids to attend to her. It gave me time to sort through my thoughts for something I could say without bursting into tears.

"If he is responsible for her disappearance, I can't imagine he would," I said. "I expect he will pretend he knows nothing. Forget he ever knew her, as he did when I asked about Nebtu."

She, too, had disappeared, although we had no information about her movements at the time.

"I wonder how long the administrators will wait before they give Lady Ishtar's chambers to someone else?" Ettu asked. "If there is anything of hers you want to keep, perhaps you should go get it, or I can go for you."

"Do you think her maids have been reassigned?" I asked.

Should I ask for Belet-ili? Did I have some obligation to her since she was sent here with me? But she didn't know about Tall and Half. Dare I risk someone else knowing, especially if that person might tell Nammu? I had no doubt Nammu still waited for a chance for revenge. She had accused me of asking my father to send Ishtar's maids to Egypt with me, and she claimed Ishtar was the one to tell her such a thing. I never did get a chance to ask my sister whether that was true. No, don't think it. She will be found yet. She will be safe. I will ask her after she is found.

When I didn't reply, Ettu looked to Merytre, who shrugged at her.

"I have only ever been reassigned because my mistress chose her favourites and didn't want me anymore," Merytre said. "Not because..."

We all knew what she avoided saying. Not because her

mistress had died. It seemed I was the only one who thought we might still find her.

"Go check on Belet-ili later this afternoon," I said. "Find out if she's heard anything about being reassigned."

"Are you thinking of bringing her back here?" Ettu asked.

I sighed, my gaze drifting over to where Half and Ahmose still talked quietly, then to Tall beside me.

"I don't know," I said. "I don't know whether we can trust her. Even if we wait until Half leaves, there is still Tall to consider. We can hardly keep him locked in a chamber all day and night so Belet-ili doesn't find out about him."

"Even if we did, it wouldn't take long before she realised something was being kept from her," Ettu said. "We would have to take food in to him and empty chamber pots. She would quickly notice something suspicious about a locked chamber that required us going in and out of it several times a day."

"Me!" Tall said rather morosely in Babylonian. He was still unable to speak Egyptian, although he understood that language probably better than any of us.

Ettu quietly translated his comment for Merytre.

"No, you aren't causing any problem." I hoped I had understood him correctly. "We will do whatever we must to keep you safe and if that means we can't bring Belet-ili here, then that's the way it will be. Besides, she has given me no reason to do her any favours."

What had I been thinking? Belet-ili was far too close to Nammu, who we definitely couldn't trust. It was Nammu who stole Tiye's jewels and told Panouk she had found them in my chambers. As best I could figure, she did it because she blamed me for my father sending her to Babylon without Ishtar.

It would only take one hint from Belet-ili for Nammu to realise something illicit occurred within my chambers. She would take great delight in going straight to the administrators with her suspicions. I couldn't afford to give Panouk or Amankhau any reason to search my chambers again.

CHAPTER 2

As the sun set, Half made his final preparations to leave. With a linen sheet wrapped around his shoulders to conceal him down to his sandals, and a scarf covering his head, he was a bizarre sight, but it was our only chance of getting him out unrecognised. If anyone noticed a strange man slipping through the hallways, there was grave danger, not only to Half, but to all of us. We were all complicit in illegally hiding two men in my chambers.

"I suppose I should be going then," Half said, directing his words to the chamber in general. "I don't know how long this mission might take. It could be merely days, or it could be weeks. I pray Marduk watches over you all in the meantime."

"Do you have a plan?" I asked, although I wasn't sure I really wanted to know. If he said no, what then? Should I tell him not to go? Could I really give up what might be my one chance to find out what had happened to Ishtar?

"I will stay out of sight as much as I can," he said. "I will seek out an unused chamber, or a quiet spot in a barn. The storage chambers at the back of the chapel, perhaps. I will only go out at night, when there are fewer people around and I am less likely to encounter Userhet or someone who would think to report my presence to him. I will listen at doors and windows, and seek information however I can. As for food, I suppose I will pilfer what I may. Sneak into the kitchens during a quiet moment; take something from a tray left outside someone's chambers. I am quite accustomed to fending for myself, so you needn't worry."

It all seemed rather uncertain to me. Hiding in some forgotten chamber during the day, and slipping out at night to spy or steal food, but I had to have confirmation of Ishtar's fate. If this was the only way to be certain of what happened to her, then I would leave Half to do as he thought best.

Before I could think of a response, Tall went to farewell Half, squeezing his shoulder with one hand and staring down at him intently. They were a strange-looking pair, a tall man and a very short one, but they had obviously become good friends in the time since we left Egypt.

"Safe!" Tall said.

"You too, buddy." Half clasped the hand on his shoulder, then turned to Ettu.

Her eyes shone, but she gave him a tight smile.

"Be careful," she said. "We will all worry for you until we see you again."

Half reached for her hand and it seemed to me he pressed something into her palm. Their hands lingered a moment longer, before Ettu pulled away. She hurried out of the sitting chamber. I assumed she wanted to shed her tears in private.

Ahmose didn't rise from her chair, but she gave Half a solemn nod. He nodded back, and although no words passed between them, I felt there was still some communication.

Perhaps it was a shared understanding of whatever Ahmose had said to him earlier.

Merytre surprised me by bending down to hug him. Although she had initially found both men rather strange, she seemed to quickly adjust to their differences. In my chambers, at least, Tall and Half were treated no differently to anyone else.

When he had finished his other farewells, Half came to stand in front of me. Tall went off to wait in the men's bedchamber and Merytre followed to lock him in. I hated that we had to do that, but it was the only way to keep him safe if someone unexpectedly came in while the sitting chamber door was open.

"My lady." Half bowed, almost losing the shawl draped over his head. Merytre returned and hurried over to adjust it for him. "I won't come back here until I have news of Lady Ishtar."

I wanted to thank him, but my throat suddenly choked and I could only incline my head in acknowledgement. Ettu returned, her eyes red but dry, and slipped out into the hallway to check whether anyone was around. She came back to gesture at Half and Merytre, indicating it was safe to leave. The women would accompany Half until he was within sight of the gates so that if anyone stopped him, they would be there to speak for him. Although we had done our best to conceal his identity, there was no way to mask his unmistakably male voice.

The door closed behind them, leaving just Ahmose and me in the sitting chamber. But before we could let Tall out, someone knocked. Ahmose and I looked at each other. Her face was as horrified as mine must surely be.

"It's too soon," I whispered. "They would have been seen in the hallway."

"I suppose all we can do is check who it is," she replied. "They will tell us soon enough if they saw something."

Normally it would be either Ettu or Merytre who would answer the door, but Ahmose was the only one left. She made her way back to the door she had just barred and cracked it open.

"It is Sehener," she said.

I let out the breath I hadn't realised I was holding. Of all my lady's maids, Sehener was the one I was most certain we could trust. She came bearing a large bunch of narcissus, their bright yellow petals gleaming like miniature suns and their stems tied with a cheery red ribbon.

"My lady," she said. "I heard about Lady Ishtar. I came to offer my condolences and to—" She stopped and swallowed hard. Her eyes glistened. "To say that if there is anything I can do for you, you have only to ask."

I tried to smile in thanks for her kind words, but my mouth wobbled and it probably looked more like a scowl. Everyone was so certain they knew Ishtar's fate, even though nobody had seen her body. Why must they all assume the worst every time another woman disappeared? Surely there were some instances in which such a disappearance had no sinister cause? I said none of that, though. Sehener's words were well-intentioned, despite how they made me feel.

"Thank you," I managed to say.

I wasn't ready for condolences. Not yet. We might still find Ishtar safe and well.

"I will take those," Ahmose said, reaching for the flowers Sehener still held.

Sehener startled as if she had forgotten them.

"Khensa said she saw you looking at some narcissus in the gardens recently," she said to me. "I thought maybe you had a particular fondness for that flower and I wanted to…" Her voice trailed away and she swallowed again.

"It was very kind of you," I said.

Sehener hesitated and the look on her face said she wanted to say something else. I waited.

"My lady," she started before hesitating. "I saw something rather strange in the hallway just now."

"This place holds many secrets." My cheeks instantly flamed and I could only hope she didn't think it was because I lied. "And some of them are more dangerous than others."

Sehener nodded, her head bobbing up and down too quickly. Perhaps she was as nervous about this conversation as I was.

"Of course it does, my lady," she said. "And I would never betray my mistress's confidence. I only hope that if you needed someone to help you keep a particular secret, you would know you can trust me."

I nodded, not trusting myself to say anything more, lest I give too much away. Sehener left without any further comment, and Ahmose closed the door behind her, sliding the bar into place with a sigh.

"Well," she said, giving me a careful look as she made her slow way back to her chair.

"I think she will hold her tongue."

"That was what she seemed to be saying, at any rate."

"You don't trust her?"

I examined Ahmose's face, but the old woman was good at keeping her thoughts to herself. She shrugged.

"Quite the contrary," she said. "Of all the maids who attend to you each morning, she is probably the first I would trust if I was inclined to trust anyone. I listen when they talk, and most of them pay no attention to an old woman like me. They say things in front of me they would never say in your hearing. But the secrets you keep are treacherous and we have tried hard to keep them within these walls."

"There are others who know," I said. "Khaemmalu and Gautseshen know about Tall and Half, and Khaemmalu knows we have left the Palace grounds. Sutem knows we had reason to install a lock, even if he doesn't know why. Tiye suspects we have been using magic of some sort, although I don't know how much she has guessed."

"The more folk who know, the higher the chance one of them will let something slip. It may not be intentional, but by that point, it won't matter. Once your secrets have been revealed, it is too late to lock them away again."

I took a deep breath, trying to steady myself. I needed to focus on Ishtar right now. I had no spare energy to worry about whether Sehener might betray me.

"It is already too late," I said. "Sehener surely saw enough to make her suspicious. We can only pray to Marduk she holds her tongue."

I went to unlock the door to the men's bedchamber. Tall followed me back out. He was silent, and although that wasn't unusual for him, I thought he looked concerned. Worried about Half, I assumed. We all were.

"The food will be getting cold," Ahmose said. She hauled herself out of her chair and shuffled over to where the servants had laid out our evening meal when they delivered it an hour ago.

She passed me a plate and offered one to Tall, but he shook

his head. The aromas from our meal were strong, and although normally I would find them enticing, all food smells made my stomach turn at the moment. I hoped it would ease soon, although Ahmose said I might continue to be sensitive to odours until my babe was born.

I took a small portion of baked fish and some salad, but set the plate aside for now. My stomach churned too ferociously to even think about eating. Instead I went to the window, hoping I might catch some glimpse of Half on his way to the gates, but the sun had finished setting and the grounds were in darkness. I looked for a while anyway, but wasn't surprised I saw no sign of three shadows slipping through the gardens.

By the time I returned to my couch, Ahmose was eating, while Tall picked at a pomegranate. I supposed he was too worried about Half to eat. I was too, and the thought of food made my stomach churn even more fiercely than the aroma did, but I made myself take a few bites. I had to keep my strength up, for the babe if not for myself.

We froze when another knock came at the door.

"It is us," came Ettu's voice and my sigh of relief was so fierce, it caught in my throat and made me cough.

Tall hurried out of the chamber while we let them in and I wondered again whether we should have sent him with Half. This was no life for a man, being forced to hide every time we opened the door for fear of someone in the hallway catching a glimpse of him. Never able to go outside in the fresh air, or to feel the sunlight on his skin. When he wanted to look outside, he had to stand next to the window where nobody would spot him. Once Half returned with news of Ishtar, I would have to send them both away. It would sadden me to do so, but there really was no other option.

When Tall returned, he flapped his hands as he studied

Ettu and Merytre, maybe looking for some indication of whether anything went wrong.

"You can stop looking at me like that," Ettu said to him. "We got him out of the building. He is hidden away near the gates to wait for the guards to open them."

"What if they don't have any reason to open the gates tonight?" I asked. "He has only one more dose of the potion."

"Merytre and I will go back in the morning and check the place we left him," she said. "If he is still there, we will figure out what to do. It might be best to leave him, though, rather than risk bringing him back inside and having to do it all again tomorrow night."

I frowned, not liking the possibility of Half spending the day hiding in the gardens, although it was probably less dangerous than parading him through the Palace again.

"Take some food with you when you go." He hadn't eaten before he left. I should have made him wait long enough to fill his belly, but food was the last thing on my mind at the time. "He will be hungry if he has been there all night."

She nodded and turned her attention to Tall, who strode up and down the chamber, flapping his hands and seeming increasingly agitated.

"He will be fine," she said, and it sounded like she was trying to convince herself as much as him. "He will be careful and he will come back as soon as he can."

"Man!" Tall said. "Belly."

"All we can do now for him is pray," Ettu said.

"Me!"

Ettu hesitated and I guessed she wasn't sure what Tall meant.

"No," I said quickly. "We can't send you as well."

"Dagger!"

"If something goes wrong, Half will come back."

But he wouldn't have made it back to us last time if Tall wasn't there. Maybe we shouldn't have sent Half after all. I prayed to Marduk that my desire for certainty about Ishtar's fate wouldn't result in Half's death.

CHAPTER 3

That night, I dreamed about lions. I was walking through the gardens. It was night and the moon was full and high in the sky. My bare feet made no more than the slightest whisper against the mud brick path. A soft breeze caressed my face and I felt completely at peace.

Then I became aware of someone following me. They were off to the side of the path, creeping through the shadows. I quickened my pace, but they kept up with me.

I called out, asking who it was, but my follower made no reply. I walked faster and still they kept pace with me. I broke into a run.

Then suddenly I was no longer on the path. Now I stood in the middle of a bed of narcissus. The flowers were all around me, only as high as my knees, but they felt like a shield.

A lion burst out of the shadows and paced around the flower bed. I stood surrounded by narcissus, and I wasn't afraid. The flowers would protect me.

The lion growled and extended one paw towards me, but

snarled and retreated, seemingly unable to pass through the flowers. A second lion joined the first and together they prowled around the flower bed. Around and around they went, searching for any weakness, but as long as the flowers were there, they couldn't get to me.

The images lingered in my mind long after I woke. The flower bed, the lions circling it but unable to cross the barrier of the flowers. How did I get into the garden? And why were the flowers protecting me? I had no answers, but the dream felt like a message.

It was only some time later as I stood at the window and tried to pretend I wasn't watching for lions, that I realised my question shouldn't have been *why* the flowers were protecting me. It should have been *how*. In my dream, it had seemed perfectly natural. I never thought to wonder how a flower could do such a thing.

After breakfast, Ettu and Merytre went to check the place where they left Half. They took a small sack of food, planning that if anyone questioned them, they would say they intended to break their fast with a picnic. They soon returned with news that he was no longer there. We could only pray to Marduk he had gotten out safely.

As I went to sit with Tiye that morning, I was still trying to shake off the dream. Making polite conversation was the last thing I felt like, but there was no point sitting in my chambers until either we received word of Ishtar or Half returned. And, as Ettu was quick to point out, if anyone had heard something about Ishtar, or about Half reappearing in Pharaoh's palace, it would be Tiye. I should be sure to visit her as often as possible while we waited for news.

Her maid, Henuttawy, let me in and Tiye was sitting on a couch looking as if she expected me.

"Oh, Kassaya," she said. "Is there any word of Ishtar?"

Her voice was sympathetic and her concern seemed genuine. Despite Ettu's earlier suspicions, I found it impossible to believe Tiye herself might be involved in making women disappear.

I sat opposite her and smoothed my skirt as I searched for something to say. To my surprise and mortification, I burst into tears.

"Oh dear," Tiye said. "Henuttawy, fetch a cloth."

She said nothing further, only waited as I cried. Henuttawy pressed a linen cloth into my hands and I wiped my face as I tried to stop my tears. My kohl was probably irretrievably smudged by now. I hated that there was no way to avoid Tiye seeing it. She herself was always immaculately presented.

"No news then, I assume?" she asked when my tears finally slowed.

I shook my head, my gaze fastened on the cloth in my hands, which was now streaked with black kohl.

Tiye gave a heavy sigh. She got to her feet and went to stand at the window. With her back to me, I couldn't tell whether she was actually looking outside or merely making a show of not looking at me. Perhaps my appearance was so terrible by now that she couldn't bear to see it.

"Kassaya," she started, but then stopped, as if undecided about whether to say whatever it was.

I sniffled and wiped my face. I was sure I would burst into tears again if I tried to say anything.

"Kassaya, this place is not what it seems," Tiye said.

"What does it seem like?" I managed to speak without sobbing, although tears welled again. I wiped them away.

"It seems like a safe place," she said. "With its high wall and the guards who patrol the grounds at all hours of the day and night. To see such things, you would think it must be the safest place in the world for a woman to live. But as you have seen, it is not."

It was no secret to anyone who lived here that women disappeared, but how much did Tiye know? Did she suspect Pharaoh's involvement?

"I think you know more than you have told me," I said.

Tiye gave me a careful look. "About Ishtar?"

"About the women who go missing."

Tiye froze at my words. I hadn't forgotten the way she reacted the last time I asked her about the missing women. *Let it go,* she had said to me. *They are gone and we are still here. Focus on that and stop poking around in matters that don't concern you.* She was probably just as likely to turn me out of her chambers as to give me any kind of answer.

She said nothing for a long time and I wondered whether this was how she would handle the situation — by simply pretending I never asked — but at length she turned back to face me. Her hand went to her throat, reminding me of the bruises I had seen on Ishtar's neck. The bruises caused by Pharaoh. She let her hand fall and gave me a shrug.

"I'm sure I hardly know what you're talking about." Her tone was dismissive, something I was beginning to suspect was Tiye's way of masking her feelings.

"I'm sure you do," I said.

"You should be careful, Kassaya." Tiye came to take her seat in front of me again. She crossed one leg over the other and smoothed her skirt before she looked at me. It was the haughty stare she used to give me when I first arrived. She hadn't looked at me like that in quite some time. "You shouldn't ask questions you don't want to hear the answers to."

"I never ask a question if I don't want the answer."

I tried to mimic her haughty look, but if she realised what I was doing, she gave no sign of it. Maybe I didn't do it properly. My cheeks heated and I looked down at my hands in my lap, hoping Tiye wouldn't notice my blush. When she still hadn't responded after a while, I darted a glance at her to find her staring at nothing, a pensive look on her face, her hand at her throat again.

"Tiye?" I asked. "Are you well?"

She started a little, as if she hadn't realised what she was doing. Her hand dropped to her lap.

"Perfectly," she said.

"Are you going to tell me what you know?"

She sighed. I'd never seen Tiye looked so discomfited, and even though I knew what I expected her to say, her obvious unease made me apprehensive.

"Kassaya, I've told you before you are too naive," she said at last. "Do you really think you can go around boldly asking questions?"

"I'm hardly going around asking questions. I'm asking you, in the privacy of your own chambers."

"Folk here don't ask questions." She looked me right in the eyes and I knew this was as much of an answer as she intended to give me. For today, at least. "It's safer that way. If you have not seen something with your own eyes, it never happened."

"Are you saying Ishtar didn't really disappear because I didn't see it?"

"You misunderstand me, and I think you do it wilfully."

Tiye broke our stare and looked down at her hands in her lap. My question had disturbed her more than I expected, but I couldn't afford to let her avoid giving me a proper answer.

Of all the women I had met since I arrived, she had lived here the longest. If anyone knew what was really going on, it was Tiye.

"I'm not trying to misunderstand you." I leaned forward and hoped the sincerity in my tone would convince her. "Truly. I just want to know what happened to Ishtar. If you know something about it, please tell me."

"There is nothing to tell."

She finally looked at me again, her usual blank expression fixed in place. I was certain she had considered telling me the truth, but the moment had passed. What a fool I was to think we had become friends. A woman like Tiye didn't have friends. She wouldn't let herself. I stood to take my leave.

"I have things to do." My tone was colder than I intended, but at least it was better than revealing how much she had hurt me by showing that what I thought was a developing friendship was nothing more than a facade.

"Kassaya, wait." Tiye gestured towards the couch. "Please."

Reluctantly, I sat and focused on arranging my skirt over my knees so I didn't have to look at her.

"I know you probably think badly of me," she said eventually. "And whether you believe it or not, I'm sorry about that. It's funny." Her voice changed, becoming more musing. "That is not something I ever thought I would say to another Ornament, but there is something about you that invites the truth. I think it's your earnestness."

"There is nothing wrong with being earnest," I muttered.

Her words stung, even though she probably meant them as a compliment. But all my life I'd been told I was different from other women. Not pretty enough. Not elegant enough. Not good enough. Tiye saying I was too earnest felt like just one more instance of that. I was too naive. I asked too many questions. I was too wilful.

"No," she said. "There is nothing wrong with it, but it's not a quality one sees much of around here."

I only shook my head. For some reason, I was about to burst into tears again. As long as I didn't speak, I could hold them back.

"Kassaya, there have been rumours," Tiye said. "Rumours which I think you need to know about, and as your friend, whether that's how you think of me or not, it behooves me to tell you."

"Like what?" At least I could say that much without crying.

"About your sister." She looked reticent now, as if she had already changed her mind about telling me.

"What about Ishtar?"

"Folk know she is missing." Tiye always spoke carefully. Purposefully. Every word she said was always exactly what she meant to say, and this was no different. "And they know the two of you argued before she disappeared."

Did she mean the way Ishtar had said I shouldn't mention Nebtu's disappearance to Pharaoh? That I endangered all of us by doing such a thing? Or did she mean the more private disagreement we had in her chambers, when she asked why I hadn't told her I was with child? Tiye looked at me steadily. I waited for her to finish, but she just gazed at me.

"Go on," I said at last.

"Kassaya, there are rumours that you had something to do with Ishtar's disappearance."

At first, I didn't understand. Her words seemed to slide into the air, disappearing into the nothingness around me. It was only when she continued to wait and watch me, that they sank in.

"Are you saying…" I stopped, but still she only looked at me. She was going to make me say it. "Do you mean folk think I killed her?"

"Some do. Others think you told her to leave. To go home, perhaps, or somewhere else. There are other rumours, of course. More ridiculous ones."

"Like what?" I held her gaze, willing her to understand I wouldn't let her get away with not telling me the truth this time. I would sit here all day if I had to.

"That you had her sold as a slave, or sent to the gold mines in Nubia."

"What?" For a few moments, I was so disconcerted, I couldn't think of any other reply, but then the words tumbled from my lips. "How would I even do such a thing? Who is saying things like that? Tell me everything you know."

She waved away my questions.

"It is ridiculous," she said. "I doubt anybody believes it. But it is well known the two of you had argued, so of course folk will talk."

"I want to know who is saying such things about me."

"Nobody you need be concerned about. It is mostly the servants. I'm sure Ornaments are talking, but not the ones who know you."

"So how do you know?"

"My maids, of course."

"Nammu?"

How much of it was even true if it came from Nammu? Where was she anyway? She was usually here when I came to visit with Tiye, lazing around and doing nothing much of anything.

"Some of it." Tiye leaned back against the couch, looking

as at ease as ever. That, it seemed, was the worst of what she intended to tell me.

"She is lying then. She blames me for her being sent here. She would do anything to make me look bad."

Like accusing me of theft.

"I wouldn't pass on anything that came from Nammu alone." Tiye gave me a reproving look. "I asked who her sources were and sent another maid to check. Nammu said other things too, much wilder claims which I have not been able to verify. Those I assume she made up and I won't share them."

I wanted to demand she tell me every last thing Nammu had said. That vexatious, spiteful shrew. Whatever she told Tiye, she had probably spread elsewhere as well. Tiye mightn't believe her, but there would be folk who did. Folk who didn't know what Nammu was like. But if Tiye said she wouldn't reveal the claims she couldn't verify, there was no point asking again.

"Thank you for telling me." I got to my feet. I needed to get out of here before I burst into tears. If I let myself cry now, I might never stop.

Tiye only nodded and gestured for Henuttawy to open the door. If she thought anything of my abrupt departure, she didn't comment on it.

CHAPTER 4

"You look upset," Ettu observed as we returned to my chambers.

I had said nothing since I emerged from Tiye's chambers, too intent on trying to keep my tears from falling. I restrained a sniffle and wondered whether to tell her. But she would probably hear the gossip herself, or Merytre would. It would be better if they heard it from me.

"I will tell you later," I said.

She nodded and didn't push.

I knew Half wouldn't have come back in the hour or two I had been gone — even if he already had news and had returned, he would wait until dark before he tried to get in through the gates — but I still found myself holding my breath as Merytre let us in.

A quick glance around the sitting chamber told me Half definitely hadn't returned. Ahmose sat in her favourite chair, a table in front of her covered with her little herb packets. Merytre shot me an assessing look as she barred the door behind us.

"Did something happen?" she asked, glancing towards Ettu as if expecting her to already know.

Ettu shrugged and went to pour herself some melon juice. She held up the jug to ask if I wanted any, but I shook my head. I took my favourite spot on the couch, trying to figure out how to tell them. Merytre went to let Tall out of the men's bedchamber. He went straight to the window and stood to the side of it as he so often did. I had the irrational thought that maybe he was looking for lions. Ettu and Merytre both sat down and looked at me expectantly.

"Go on then," Ettu said. "What is it?"

"Tiye told me about some rumours," I said.

Maybe they had already heard, but if any of them knew what I was about to say, they gave no sign of it. I wished I had more time to figure out how to say it. My thoughts were jumbled and I knew it would come out all wrong, but at least the tears seemed to have stopped. I should tell them while I could say it.

"She said some folk blame me for Ishtar's disappearance." I knew it would be painful to say, but even so, the words hurt more than I expected. My eyes stung and I blinked back the tears.

"What cheek," Ettu said indignantly. "How dare Lady Tiye say such a thing."

"She is not the one saying it," I said. "She just thought I should know. And I do appreciate her telling me." The words came out in a rush. "I would rather know than not."

"Folk here are quick to gossip," Merytre said with a shrug. "There are probably all sorts of reasons for her disappearance being discussed. Remember it wasn't all that long ago folk were saying Lady Tiye had something to do with making certain women disappear."

"Nasty!" Tall said with a frown. He turned to glance at us, then returned his gaze to the window.

"Yes, they are nasty," Ettu said. "And very insensitive. How anyone could even think such a thing, I don't know."

"Is there anything I can do about it?" I asked.

My gaze wandered to Ahmose. She was the only one who hadn't commented yet. She met my eyes with her usual placid look.

"As Merytre says, folk will gossip in a place like this," she said. "Most of them probably don't believe it, but it gives them something exciting to share. You shouldn't let it bother you."

"How do I stop it from bothering me? She is my sister, and she may be..." My voice choked as a sob burst out. "And folk think..."

"Nobody who knows you would think such a thing," Ettu said. "You must remember that. I can talk to your lady's maids if you want. Make sure they know they are to refute it if they hear any such gossip. I'm sure they would do so anyway. You know they think very highly of you. They have said before you only have to tell them what you want folk to know and they will tell everyone."

"I won't counter gossip with more gossip. How would that help?"

"Because it allows you to correct the misinformation." Ettu's voice was stiff and I realised with a pang I had hurt her feelings.

"I know you're trying to help." It was the closest I could come to an apology right now. "But I don't like being gossiped about and I don't want to fuel it."

"That is how a place like this functions, though," she said. "Folk spread the news of what is happening, or what they want others to *think* is happening. There is not an Ornament here who wouldn't take the chance to correct such gossip if it's not what she wants people saying about her."

"Except me." My cheeks felt wet and I wiped them, surprised to find I must have been crying while she was talking. So much for holding back my tears.

"Except you," she said.

I had forgotten Ahmose's presence until she cleared her throat. She fiddled with her herbs while she considered her words. She seemed to be transferring herbs from larger packets into the little ones I was more used to seeing. Perhaps she had just recently restocked, although she surely would have mentioned it if she had been able to source the special ingredient for her invisibility potion.

"Perhaps you don't need to involve so many folk," she said.

"What do you mean?" I asked.

"It would only take one or two people with different information to share to refute the rumours." Ahmose's voice was as calm as ever.

"I could do it," Merytre said.

"As could I," Ettu added.

"No, not you." Merytre frowned at her. "Everyone knows how close you are to my lady. They might not believe you in the way they would believe me."

"You are close to her too," Ettu pointed out. "She has only two lady's maids who have their own chambers in her suite."

"That is different," Merytre said. "You arrived with her. You're both Babylonian. It's clear to everyone you have a bond with her that the rest of us don't. Folk would think you biased. Me, though. I could say just about anything and because I too have my own chamber, folk would think I have private information. They would believe me."

"No," I said. "I won't be a party to spreading gossip, especially gossip about myself."

Doing such a thing felt wrong. Shameful, or perhaps shameless. It would make me a person I didn't want to be.

Merytre shrugged and appeared unbothered. Ettu seemed to be carefully controlling her face, although the stiffness in her shoulders said she was still unhappy.

"I will ignore it," I said. "Unless someone asks me directly, of course. But if anyone stopped to think about it, they would surely realise it makes no sense. How would I even—" My voice broke and I stopped to compose myself. "How would I even do such a thing? How would I make a woman — any woman — disappear and cover it up? I would need…"

"Alliances," Ettu said. "A network."

"Men willing to remove a body and dispose of it," Merytre added.

"And I have none of that," I said.

"Actually, you do," Ettu said. "You have an alliance with Lady Tiye."

"A network with your maids," Merytre said.

"And both Khaemmalu and Sutem have been willing to help us with things they shouldn't," Ettu concluded.

They were right. I hadn't realised it before. Had only been thinking about the kind of alliances Tiye must have. Mine were surely paltry compared to hers, but Ettu and Merytre were correct that I had my own alliances.

"Surely that doesn't mean anyone would believe I could be capable of something like…" I couldn't make myself say it.

"They won't," Ettu said. "Think of how the Ornaments reacted to the matter of Lady Tiye's stolen jewels. You told us most of them said they never believed it of you."

"That was only a small group of women," I said. "Friends of

Tiye, to whom she would surely have told the truth, and they aren't representative of what everyone else thinks."

"Why does everyone else matter?" Ettu asked. "There are thousands of women living in this place and I'm sure you haven't so much as seen the faces of most of them, let alone actually met them. So why does the opinion of strangers matter so much to you?"

"I don't know." Frustration surged, although I knew it was with myself rather than with her. As usual, Ettu's comments were perfectly sensible. "It just does."

Ettu shrugged and went to stand next to Tall at the window. He had said nothing past that one interjection. Maybe he wasn't even listening anymore. The matter of women's gossip might be irrelevant to him. They were women he didn't know, after all, and he wasn't likely to ever meet any of them.

As my emotions calmed, I tried to understand why I was so frustrated. It wasn't the first time folk had gossiped about me. The theft of Tiye's jewels was one thing, but even back in Babylon, there had been those who liked to spread rumours about me. I had always felt different to other women. Set apart from them somehow. They never liked me and were only too quick to talk when I did something they didn't approve of, such as befriend a person they considered an outsider, like Tall or Half.

The suggestion that I spread my own gossip wasn't all that unreasonable, but gossip was hurtful. Hateful. I knew just how cruel it could be. I'd always hated gossip and it didn't seem right to be the one who spread it, even if it was to benefit myself. Perhaps especially if it was to benefit myself.

Since Ettu had started dressing like a man, she had been filled with a confidence I didn't have and I envied her for it.

She strode along the palace hallways wearing her *shendyt*, and paid not the slightest attention to the women who whispered and sniggered in her wake. How did she do it? And did she really not care what they thought, or was it a pretence? Either way, she certainly gave the impression she cared nothing for what they said about her.

Tiye was the same. She guarded her position as Pharaoh's Favourite, but she was completely unbothered about what anyone else thought of her. How did some women gain such confidence and others, like me, didn't?

I wished I could be more like them. Then maybe knowing that folk spread such vicious lies about me wouldn't hurt quite so much.

CHAPTER 5

Tiye's comments lingered on my mind for the rest of the day. Ettu was probably right that nobody who knew me would actually believe I had anything to do with Ishtar's disappearance. I pondered the suggestion that I let my maids spread a different tale, but couldn't quite bring myself to do it. Surely there was a better way to manage such a situation.

There had been no word from Half, not that I expected to hear from him until he returned, but there must be something I could do in the meantime to seek out information about Ishtar. I paced the sitting chamber as I tried to come up with a solution. There was only one thing I could think of, although it would undoubtedly stir up even more gossip. Someone needed to do it, though, and it should be me. I should have thought of it earlier.

"I'm going to search Ishtar's chambers," I said.

Ettu and Merytre had been chatting quietly while they worked on their stitching. Ahmose was relaxing in her favourite chair and Tall was at the window. They all turned to look at me.

"Do you think Panouk will let you?" Ettu asked, setting her stitching aside.

"Does he even need to know?" I countered. "As long as one of her maids is there to let me in, why would I need to ask him?"

"You intend to demand her maids let you in, and then what?" she asked. "Go through her chambers? Hope to stumble on some clue that might reveal what happened to her?"

That was exactly what I had thought, although it sounded rather daft when she said it. She would know if I lied to her, though. Searching for a truthful response, I cast my gaze around the chamber and my eyes met Ahmose's. The look she gave me was as unperturbed as ever.

"If you weren't already quite certain of her fate, you wouldn't have sent Half to Pharaoh's palace," she said.

It was true, but I couldn't let go of the idea I might find something. Some clue everyone else had missed. Something that might tell us she left of her own accord after all. I finally found an answer to Ettu's question.

"Yes." I got to my feet. "That is exactly what I'm going to do. Are you coming with me?"

Ettu sighed. "I suppose someone has to."

"I will," Merytre offered.

"We may as well both go," Ettu said.

At Ishtar's chambers a short while later, Ettu rapped on the door. It was Belet-ili who answered and she gave me a frosty look.

"My lady would like to inspect Lady Ishtar's chambers," Ettu said.

Belet-ili made no move to let us in.

"Why?" she asked.

"In case there is something here to explain what happened to her," I said.

"You already know what happened," she replied, and her tone was no less frosty than her glare. "She went to Pharaoh's palace and she never came back."

"Belet-ili, I know she means a lot to you," I said. "But she is my sister. Maybe there is nothing here to give us any information, but I have to try."

Her fingers twitched on the door, as if she considered letting me in.

"Please," I said.

Belet-ili sighed and opened the door wider, then retreated without a word.

I'd only been inside Ishtar's chambers once — the time I visited her after we both fell sick while dining with Pharaoh. The time she told me she had lost her babe. I hadn't taken much notice of the details back then, but now I studied the fine furnishings, the woven rugs and elegant tapestries. I saw nothing of my sister in her surroundings.

Panouk had told me when I first arrived that my chambers could be redecorated in any way I wanted. I assumed he must have offered the same to Ishtar, but I saw no hand of hers in the furnishings. Perhaps her surroundings were elegant enough that she felt no need to change them. Or perhaps she never intended to be here long enough for it to matter.

"I suppose her bedchamber would be the most logical place to start," Ettu said.

Belet-ili only pointed us towards a door, then went to sit down. It was clear she intended to give no aid to our search.

"Where are the rest of Ishtar's maids?" I asked.

Belet-ili shrugged. "They left."

"Have they been reassigned?"

Another shrug.

"Have you told Panouk they don't come to her chambers anymore?" I kept my tone calm and tried to hide my frustration at her unhelpfulness.

"Why bother?" Belet-ili shot back. "Lady Ishtar is not here so it matters little whether her maids come or not."

I wondered why she herself was here, but didn't ask. I had already antagonised her enough.

Ishtar's bedchamber was much smaller than mine and felt crowded with Ettu, Merytre and I.

"What are we looking for?" Merytre asked.

"Anything that might explain what happened," I said. "Maybe something that gives us a clue as to her intentions."

As if we didn't already know what had happened to her. As if she had some control over her fate. It was only as I stood here in her bedchamber that I realised why I had really come. I had thought I would sense her here. Feel some connection to her. I had thought that if my sister was still alive, I would stand in her chambers and know it. But like her sitting chamber, I felt nothing of my sister here.

Ishtar's bedchamber was tidy, the blanket folded on the end of the bed, and her clothes neatly laid out in storage chests. On the dresser, her cosmetics stood in orderly rows and a small crate contained her jewels. Her makeup looked much the same as mine, little clay bottles and boxes of lip colour, kohl and rouges.

As I rummaged through her jewels, I recognised one pendant as something I had seen her wearing. Some pretty gem-studded hair clips also looked familiar. At the bottom of the crate, my fingers encountered something wrapped in linen. Inside, was a red gem, the size of a hen's egg and polished to perfection. A silver setting surrounded it, with a cord to be worn around the neck.

"Oh my," Ettu said from beside me.

At her exclamation, Merytre came to see what I had found.

"Do you think that is from Pharaoh?" she asked.

"It must be the gift he sent when she told him she was with child," I said.

He sent me a blue sapphire, although my gem was considerably smaller. So Pharaoh favoured Ishtar even in his gift. Despite the extravagance of the robin egg sized gem he gave me, I had known hers would be even grander. Before I could think too hard about it, I rewrapped the gem and tucked it into my pouch.

"You should take all her jewels," Ettu said. "Otherwise the administrators will, and they will give them to some other Ornament. Even if you don't want to wear them, they might be useful in some other way."

We found nothing else of interest in her chambers and nothing to suggest Ishtar had planned to leave. I called Belet-ili to go through the clothing chests and see if anything was missing, but there were too many clothes, and if anything wasn't there, she couldn't identify them.

"If she had planned to leave that day, surely she would have taken her jewels," Ettu said.

It was a sensible, and rather obvious, suggestion. Pharaoh's gem alone would have provided her with an extravagant lifestyle. Any woman who was in possession of such a thing, and who planned to flee, would take it with her. If Belet-ili noticed the crate of jewels in Ettu's arms as we left, she said nothing.

On our way back to my chambers, we turned a corner and came face-to-face with Nammu.

"Greetings, Nammu," Ettu said in the tone she used when she was determined to be amiable.

Nammu didn't respond. She didn't even look at us as she made to move around us.

"Why are you spreading rumours that I was responsible for my sister's disappearance?" The words came out of my mouth before I thought about it. There was no point confronting Nammu. She would neither confess, nor change her behaviour. All it would do was antagonise her.

Nammu stopped walking and met my eyes. Her glare burned as she gave me a disdainful sniff.

"You were always jealous of her," she said. "Everyone could see it, even Lady Ishtar."

"That is nonsense."

It was true, though, wasn't it? How many times had I thought about how everyone said Ishtar was the beautiful sister, the elegant one, the witty one. The one expected to marry a king.

"I suppose you're feeling very pleased with yourself now," Nammu continued. "You finally got her out of the way and now you can have all the attention to yourself."

"Nammu, that is—"

But she was already gone, striding away down the hallway fast enough to make it clear she had no intention of conversing further with me.

CHAPTER 6

I had noticed Tall shooting me anxious looks for several days before he finally caught me alone in the sitting chamber. Ettu had gone to put away my clean laundry which had just been delivered and I had sent Merytre for a walk so she would stop standing at the window and sighing at Sutem's absence from her view.

Ahmose had disappeared on some errand of her own, most likely something to do with her herbs, although I knew she probably wasn't trying to get more of the special one she used for the invisibility potion. It was too dangerous at the moment with the butler, Weren, sniffing around for evidence of magic use. Tall came to sit beside me and flapped his hands as he studied my face.

"What is it?" I asked.

He looked away, over to the other side of the chamber, and continued his flapping.

"Tall?" I set my hand to his knee, meaning to reassure him that whatever it was, I would listen, but he let out a startled cry and jumped up. I had again forgotten he didn't like to be touched if he wasn't the one to initiate the contact. I must try harder to remember.

"I'm sorry," I said. "Please come back."

He studied me warily, as if unsure whether he could trust me.

"I promise I won't do it again," I said.

He considered that for a few moments before returning to sit beside me.

"Is there something you want to tell me?" My fingers itched to touch him — cover his hand perhaps — and I restrained myself.

"Pharaoh!" he said at last. "Danger!"

I sighed heavily. "You were trying to tell me, but I didn't listen."

I met his eyes, noting the sorrow in them. How painful must it be for him to know such a thing and be unable to communicate it? I had always been rather proud I listened to him — that I didn't assume he was an idiot because of his limited ability to communicate — but was I really any better than anyone else? Twice now, Tall had tried to tell me something important and I hadn't listened well enough to understand him.

"I'm sorry," I said. "Truly."

He looked away, nodded, flapped his hands.

"Tall, how did you find out about Pharaoh? About the things he does."

His gaze darted back to meet mine ever so briefly.

"Man!" he said.

"A man told you?"

He shook his head and flapped his hands faster.

"It is all right," I said. "Try again. How did you know?"

His mouth worked, searching for the word he wanted, and my heart ached at how vulnerable he looked.

"Ears," he said at last.

"You heard something." I had already guessed as much.

"Me! Idiot!"

"Someone said something in front of you, thinking you wouldn't understand?"

Or perhaps they assumed he wouldn't be able to tell anyone what he heard.

His shoulders slumped as he nodded. His mind was no less sharp than anyone else's and he must find such assumptions painful.

"What can you tell me about the man you heard?" I asked. "Do you know his name?"

"Pharaoh! Danger!"

"Yes, I know," I said soothingly. "I believe you, but I need you to tell me how you know."

"Pharaoh!" He stared intently into my eyes, as if trying to send the words straight into my mind.

"Who told you about Pharaoh?"

"Pharaoh!" His tone had turned to frustration now. He jumped up and paced the chamber, flapping his hands furiously. "Pharaoh! Pharaoh! Pharaoh!"

And once again, I realised I hadn't listened properly. I heard the words he said, but I didn't really listen. I did what I so often did when talking with Tall: I assumed the words he managed to say were not the ones he wanted to say. But perhaps sometimes they were.

"Tall, do you mean it was Pharaoh you heard?" I asked.

He rushed back to sit beside me, his face hopeful now.

"Pharaoh!" he said. "Guard! Woman!"

Bit by bit, I managed to draw the details out of him. He

had overheard Pharaoh telling one of his guards — a man Tall knew as Hori, presumably Pharaoh's captain or his second — to remove a woman's body. It had been some months ago, from what I could make out. Too late to have been the servant woman, Kawit, who disappeared shortly before we arrived in Egypt. So she must be another woman who had disappeared and who we had heard nothing of.

My heart hurt at knowing Tall had tried to tell me weeks ago about the danger posed by Pharaoh. If I had listened to him, I could have warned Ishtar. I could have sent her away — not back to Babylon maybe, but somewhere else. Anywhere. She could have used Ahmose's potion to get out of the Palace. I could have sent a message to Tall and Half to find her and go with her. Half would never have been stabbed, and Ishtar would be safe.

But she wouldn't have left, not willingly. Not while she was so favoured by Pharaoh and while there was talk she might edge Tiye out of her position as Favourite. Even if I had known with certainty what her fate would have been, could I really have done anything to save her? Or did I needlessly torture myself with the pretence I could have?

"I'm sorry, " I said again. "I didn't listen, did I?"

He gave me a little twisted smile that didn't quite reach his eyes. It wasn't just Ishtar and Half I had let down. It was Tall as well.

"I promise I will do better," I said.

He nodded and looked away. His mouth worked as he tried to say something else.

"Queen!" he said at last and gave me a sorrowful look.

I sighed and reached for his hand, before remembering he didn't like to be touched unexpectedly.

"I know," I said, clasping my hands in my lap so I wouldn't do it again. "You tried to tell me. I didn't listen then either."

"Me!"

I studied his face, looking for some clue as to what he meant.

"You think it's your fault?" I asked.

He nodded and flapped his hands.

"Idiot!"

"Tall, you are not an idiot, no matter what anyone says. You're just different and folk can be cruel to those who are different. But look at you. You're loyal and true, and those people who mock you would be lucky to have a friend half as good as you."

"Buddy!"

"You're worried about Half?"

"Userhet! Belly!"

"I know. I'm worried Userhet will see him too. Half will be doing everything he can to ensure he is not seen any more than necessary. You know he planned to only go out at night."

But folk would talk as soon as he was spotted in Pharaoh's palace. Their departure had been sudden enough to prompt speculation that reached even Tiye. Folk would talk no less at his reappearance, and the fact that Tall hadn't returned with him. Half's plan had involved staying hidden as much as he could, but surely there would be people who saw him. He would learn nothing if he never spoke to anyone.

"We must pray he is safe," I said. "Pray to Marduk or whoever you worship that the gods will protect Half until he is able to come back to us."

Marduk hadn't done much to protect him last time, though. Perhaps I should pray to the Egyptian goddess, Isis. I would pray she wrapped her wings of protection around Half, as Ahmose had told me she could.

CHAPTER 7

One day faded slowly into another. A week passed since Ishtar had disappeared, then another, and still there was no news. No information about my sister. No message from Half. Nothing from the administrators. When I left my chambers, folk no longer asked after her. It was as if she had simply vanished. Or had never been here.

Even Tiye didn't mention her again. It was only within the privacy of my own chambers that anyone spoke of her. I supposed everyone else assumed she was dead and that I would come to realise it sooner or later. Tiye certainly did. She had told me as much the day I asked if she had a way of finding out whether Ishtar ever reached Pharaoh's palace that night.

The silence was slowly suffocating me. Every time I thought about Ishtar, my chest tightened and my heart raced. Waves of panic crashed over me, again and again, until I felt like I would go mad. If I was lying down when it started, it felt like I was suffocating. I would dive out of bed and fling open the window shutters. A couple of times, I'd spent half the night standing at the window, gulping in the night air and trying to find a way to breathe through the panic.

Today, I'd spent the afternoon on the couch in the sitting chamber, trying to ignore the tightness in my chest and the shortness of my breath, and I couldn't bear the thought of sitting here a moment longer. The days were still hot, although surely the season of *akhet* was almost at its end. It would be *peret* soon, if I remembered correctly, and the days would start to cool.

The heat seemed to be affecting everyone today, making us all lazy. Tall lay on a couch with his eyes closed. I couldn't tell whether he was actually sleeping, but he had neither moved nor spoken in some time. Ettu and Merytre were in their favourite chairs. Ettu was pretending to work on some stitching, although she hadn't made any obvious progress today, at least as far as I could see, while Merytre seemed to be doing nothing more than daydreaming. About Sutem, probably. Ahmose's face bore a contemplative look, which probably meant she was busy thinking about herbs or potions or some such thing.

It was almost dusk and I couldn't possibly spend the evening in the same way as the day. I was also itching to talk to Ahmose, but didn't want the others to hear me.

"I'm going for a walk," I said, getting to my feet.

Ettu immediately set aside her stitching.

"I will come with you," she said.

"No, stay," I said. "Ahmose will accompany me."

Ettu raised her eyebrows, but didn't comment, only took up her needlework again. I didn't miss the disappointed look that crossed Merytre's face, although she said nothing. She was surely hoping to come with me in case we ran into Sutem.

Ahmose rose with a groan which made me feel bad about my request. But I might have to wait for days if I wanted to speak privately with her, given how much time we all spent in the sitting chamber. Neither she nor I spoke as we made our way down the three flights of stairs to the ground level.

In the gardens, the air was hot and still. My chambers were high enough to catch the breezes that wafted over the walls surrounding the Palace, but down here, there wasn't even the slightest gasp of wind. The sun scalded my skin as I led Ahmose towards a path shaded by large acacia trees. Their branches provided welcome relief from the sun's rays. It was only once we were well away from the Palace that Ahmose spoke.

"I assume there is something you wish to discuss in private," she said.

"Yes, and it really couldn't wait any longer."

We walked a little further while I tried to find the right words. I should have been planning what I would say to her as we came out, but instead I'd been in a mindless daze, too thankful that the act of moving had quelled the waves of panic to think about anything else.

"I need you to help me become powerful," I said at last. "Regardless of Ishtar's situation" — regardless of whether she was found alive, was what I really meant — "Pharaoh needs to be held accountable for his crimes."

"Pharaoh cannot commit a crime." Ahmose's voice was mild. "He is above the law. There is not a person in Egypt who would try to hold him accountable for his actions, dastardly as they might be."

"Might be?" I shot her an aghast look. "Ahmose, he is a murderer. And not just once, but many times over. We have no idea how many times he has done it."

"It is truly terrible," she said. "I only mean for you to understand there is no process within the law to hold Pharaoh to account for such a thing. No police chief will arrest him. No magistrate will try him. So long as he exists in this mortal realm, he is beyond reproach. It is the gods themselves who will judge him, and only once he travels to Osiris's Hall. There, he will be questioned in front of the forty-two judges and they will decide whether his actions were justified. There, his heart will be weighed against the Feather of Truth, and if his heart is the heavier, it will be eaten by the Devourer, and he will cease to exist."

I was passingly familiar with what the Egyptians believed about the judgement they expected to face after death. It had been the subject of one of Ahmose's lessons as we sailed from Babylon. It surprised me somewhat to learn that even Pharaoh — he who was considered more than merely a mortal man — would be subjected to this same judgement. And yet he was supposed to become a star in the sky. Perhaps that was after his judgement, and only if his heart wasn't eaten.

But despite the Egyptian beliefs, I couldn't accept allowing Pharaoh to continue murdering innocent women until he finally died. As if the magnitude of Pharaoh was too great for anything else. As if the lives of the women he killed meant nothing.

I couldn't trust the gods to punish him when he reached the afterlife. Would he be permitted to defend himself? To justify his actions? What if they accepted his excuses and didn't allow the Devourer, whatever manner of monstrous creature that might be, to eat his heart? I needed to see justice done in this lifetime. For Ishtar, and for all the other women he had killed.

"It is not enough," I said. "I will not live in fear. Pharaoh needs to be held accountable."

"What do you propose then?" Ahmose asked.

"I want to be powerful. I want Pharaoh to fear me."

We walked in silence as she considered this. The path wound through a place where the acacia were planted further apart and I noticed the sun had started to set. We must have been walking for longer than I realised. We should turn back. Ahmose was too old for such a long walk, and she sounded somewhat breathless, but I needed to know if she could help me.

"I do not know that kind of spell," Ahmose said at last. "And I cannot even begin to think how one would go about creating such a thing."

She forestalled my comment with an upraised finger.

"But I do know someone who might be able to help," she added.

"No," I said quickly. "Nobody must know. It is too dangerous."

The penalties for breaking the rules here were excessively harsh. Tall and Half would have been executed if they were discovered within the Palace grounds, and all because Pharaoh had decided no unmodified men may enter. An Ornament caught having an affair would be burned alive and her lover thrown to the crocodiles. Ettu was threatened with being sent to the gold mines, and me with her, when she was falsely accused of having stolen Tiye's gems. The punishment for treason would undoubtedly be far more severe than any other penalty I had heard of.

"You cannot tell anyone," I said.

"I will be discreet," Ahmose replied. "I won't say exactly what I seek, or why, but I don't have the knowledge to achieve what you want on my own. If you want to do this, you must trust me to find the information I need."

CHAPTER 8

$\mathcal{I}$ was still trying to think of a way to impress on Ahmose that she needed to be extremely cautious in how she sought the information I requested when a nearby bush rustled. Khaemmalu stepped out and my breath caught in my throat. How much had he heard? So far, he had given me no reason to mistrust him, but the secrets he already knew were nothing like this one. This might be beyond what even Khaemmalu would hide for me. But if he had heard anything of our conversation, he gave no sign of it.

"My lady," he said, inclining his head towards me. "Old Mother," to Ahmose. "May I walk with you, Lady Kassaya?"

"Of course." My cheeks heated and I prayed the encroaching darkness would hide them. I always responded too enthusiastically when he asked to accompany me. I should be more careful, lest he start thinking I desired an affair with him.

Khaemmalu came to walk beside me and Ahmose dropped back behind us. We followed the path as it led away from the acacias, winding now between bushes and garden beds. A light breeze whisked away the aroma of the flowers, and somewhere nearby, an owl hooted twice before falling silent. The gardens at night, even so early in the evening, felt like an entirely different world from the gardens during the day.

"Is it not too early for you to be on duty?" I asked, feeling like one of us should try to make conversation.

"A little," he said. "I started early tonight."

"I see." I couldn't think of any other reply.

"There is no word of your sister?" Khaemmalu asked.

A sigh burst out of me and I shook my head. My throat choked and for one horrifying moment, I thought I would burst into tears in front of him. He said nothing and didn't even look at me, only continued his unhurried pace while I composed myself.

"The information from your friend was the last we heard," I said. "I don't suppose he has told you anything else?"

It was through his friend who worked in Pharaoh's personal squad that we had confirmed Ishtar did indeed reach Pharaoh that night. Khaemmalu shook his head.

"No, although I have seen him twice since then," he said. "He is listening for word of her, but has heard nothing. I'm afraid that is not unusual in a case like this." His voice was gentle now, as if he feared I would shatter into pieces if he said the wrong thing. "When a woman vanishes, her disappearance is total. I've never known a situation where someone later says they saw her, or a friend hears from her. They are gone and are never heard from again."

"The administrators usually say the woman has returned to her family. Have you never known that to happen?"

"I'm afraid not, and some of the missing women have families here in Thebes. We would know if they had indeed gone back to their fathers."

"So there really is no hope," I said. "For Ishtar."

"I'm sorry." He stopped walking and turned to face me. "Both for Lady Ishtar and for you. But we know enough to be quite certain of her fate, and indeed, she has been gone for too long. If she had merely run off, she would have sent word to you by now. She would know you are worried about her."

She wouldn't have left. Not while she was so close to becoming Pharaoh's Favourite, and not without telling me. But hearing Khaemmalu say it somehow made it more real. It was now a solid thing. A fact. Ishtar was dead. There was no point searching for information because we would never find anything, and Half had needlessly risked his life by returning to Pharaoh's palace. My sister was really, truly gone.

Waves of panic crashed over me. My chest was tight, my sight blurred, and for a time I knew nothing other than the feelings flooding me. When I came back to my senses, Khaemmalu was gripping both my shoulders.

"Lady Kassaya," he was saying. "Kassaya, I am here. You are safe."

I met his eyes and the concern in them made me burst into tears. His fingers on my shoulders tightened and for a moment I thought he would draw me close. Wrap his arms around me. But then I remembered. I was an Ornament and Khaemmalu already risked his life by touching me even as he was. He could not embrace me, no matter how much I wanted him to.

Although it hurt even more to do it, I stepped back. He let go of my shoulders and held up his hands, studying them, as if wondering whether it was really his own hands which had so firmly grasped me. It was against the rules. A crime, I supposed. Because Pharaoh said it was, and Pharaoh was the law. We both knew the penalty for such a thing.

"I'm sorry," I said, although I hardly knew what I apologised for.

"No, it is I who am sorry," he said. "I shouldn't have touched you."

My eyes met his and the shadowy world around us faded away. There was nothing in this moment but he and I.

"I'm glad you did." The words fell out of my mouth, but it was too late to try to pretend I didn't mean what it sounded like. From the way Khaemmalu stiffened, it was clear he didn't misunderstand me.

The air between us was charged and he seemed to sway just the slightest bit towards me. His gaze drifted down to my mouth. Was he thinking about kissing me? Then he shook his head and the moment was lost.

"I must continue with my rounds," he said as he took a step back. Away from me. "I will get a message to you if my friend hears anything further about Lady Ishtar."

I nodded, too disappointed in the loss of whatever might have been between us to trust myself to speak. I was horribly afraid that if I said anything right now, it might be to beg him to kiss me.

CHAPTER 9

From the window in my sitting chamber, I looked down on the gardens three stories below me, searching for something to distract me from last night's conversation with Khaemmalu and the way his gaze had lingered on my mouth. I raised my hand to my lips and touched them gently. What would it feel like if he kissed me? I couldn't even begin to guess. How did one know what a kiss felt like if one had never experienced such a thing?

"My lady, are you well?" Ettu asked from her chair.

I tried to shake off the lingering memory and appear more normal. Thank Marduk it wasn't Ettu who came with me last night. She would be sure to guess my thoughts. Ahmose, too, might well guess, but unlike Ettu, she was unlikely to comment on it unless invited to. She had gone out immediately after breakfast, anyway, and hadn't yet returned. I hoped she was searching for a way to make me powerful.

"Well enough," I said, returning my attention to the grounds three stories below us.

A woman slowly made her way along a path, trailed by

two maids. From this distance, I couldn't tell who she was. Neferu perhaps. She gestured towards a flower bed and one of her maids darted forward to pluck some flowers. So Neferu, if indeed it was her, would have a fresh bouquet in her chambers today.

There was something cheerful about a vase of flowers, even though their fragrance irritated my nose. I had only been able to tolerate the narcissus Sehener brought me for a couple of days. Their heady scent had filled the sitting chamber, leaving me with both a headache and a runny nose until Ettu disposed of them without comment, probably because she tired of hearing my sniffs. As if thinking of her had brought her to my side, Ettu came to stand next to me. Her gaze surveyed the grounds, perhaps wondering whether I watched something in particular.

"Perhaps you should host a dinner for the Ornaments," she suggested. "It would give you the chance to correct the rumours Lady Tiye mentioned."

"I don't think now is the right time," I said. "How can I have a party when we still have no confirmation about what happened to Ishtar? If folk already gossip about me, think what they would say when they heard that."

"It would be a distraction."

"It would look presumptuous." As if I thought these women I hardly knew were my friends, despite the secret "business" they wouldn't share with me. "And unfeeling."

As if I didn't care that Ishtar was still missing. It was hardly likely to be those women who were gossiping about me anyway.

"Then how about a walk?" Ettu suggested. "I will come with you. I finished that extra shirt I was working on for Half this morning, so I have nothing else to do."

"I hope he is safe."

The words were out of my mouth before I thought better of it. Ettu must be worried about him too, even more than me. It had been little more than a week since he left. Not very long at all really. He had said he might be gone for several days, or even for weeks. It might be some time yet before we could expect to hear from him.

"That is the first time you have mentioned him since he left." Ettu's voice was studiously casual as she stared out the window, although her gaze was too high for her to be looking at anything in the grounds. "I was wondering whether you had forgotten him."

"Forgotten Half? Of course not. It's just I know you must be worried and I didn't want to make it worse by talking about him."

She ran her fingers over the window sill as if checking whether it needed dusting.

"Feeling like I can't talk about him makes it worse," she said.

"But of course you can. We are all worried for him."

"What if…" Her voice trailed away and when I glanced at her again, she was wiping away a tear. I pretended not to notice. "What if Userhet has seen him? Once he realises he didn't succeed in killing Half last time, he will undoubtedly try again. And if that happens, we probably won't even hear of it. They will take care to cover it well."

It was true, of course. If something happened to Half, we might never know. It wasn't as if anyone would send me a message to say he had been killed by one of Pharaoh's own men.

"I don't know what to say to ease your mind," I confessed. "We can only pray that Marduk returns him safely to us."

"I'm not so sure I believe in Marduk anymore."

I couldn't have been more surprised at her words and it took me a few moments to find a reply.

"Why not?" I asked.

"The people here have different gods. They look different; they have different characteristics. I have tried to find something I recognise in the Egyptian gods, but they are so foreign to me. It makes me think maybe the gods don't really exist."

"Maybe there are many gods," I said. "Or they are all aspects of the same gods."

"Or we made them up because we needed something to believe in. Something more powerful than ourselves."

"Is that really what you think?" I asked.

In the gardens down below, Neferu or whoever it was, had circled around and headed back towards the Palace. Her maids trailed a little further behind her now. Maybe their legs were tired. She had walked quite a long way. I finally realised Ettu hadn't replied and when I glanced at her, she was still staring out the window. Her eyes glistened.

"Is this really about the gods?" I asked.

She let out a long sigh and shrugged.

"I don't know," she said. "I feel so confused. All my life, I have been told the gods watched over us. That they ensure everything happens as it should. Then we came here and folk say it is Pharaoh who controls everything. Yet he is no more than a mortal child when he is born. I don't know what to believe."

"That confuses me too," I confessed. "I don't understand how a child born of a mortal woman can become a god."

It suddenly hit me. If my son did somehow become heir, and then one day Pharaoh, he too would become a god. I would be the mother of a god. Ettu must have realised the same thing, because she gave me a wide-eyed look.

"Do you realise—" she started.

"I just—" I said at the same time.

"Your babe," she said.

My mind whirled. I couldn't fathom such a thing. How could my babe that I carried in my belly become a god?

"Maybe it's something you have to grow up with," Ettu said. "Maybe we can never truly understand because it's not what we knew as children."

"Perhaps." Every story I knew of Marduk said he had always been a god. He fought against other gods to rise to prominence over them, but we had no tales that suggested he had ever been mortal. None that I had ever heard, at any rate. "You could ask Ahmose. She is very knowledgeable and surely understands it better than we do. She would be able to explain."

"Half thinks highly of her knowledge," Ettu said. "He says she is the wisest person he has ever met, man or woman."

"I'm very glad we have her with us."

Indeed, there was so much we couldn't have done without Ahmose. It was her potions that got us out of the gates unseen. Without her, we couldn't have communicated with Tall and Half while they were in Pharaoh's palace, and they wouldn't have been able to get to us after Half was stabbed. He would have died without Gautseshen to stitch him together and Ahmose to ensure the wound didn't turn bad afterwards.

She had made another potion, too, a special one for me to put in Pharaoh's wine to increase the likelihood of him getting me with child. I thanked Marduk for her foresight every time I thought of it. Because of that, I hadn't had to suffer Pharaoh lying with me again. Not yet, anyway. I supposed that once my son was delivered, I might have to. Pharaoh would surely want another child from me as soon as possible.

My gaze went to the tray containing the barley and wheat seeds. Only the barley had sprouted after I urinated on them, signalling my babe would be a boy. The stalks were young yet, vivid green and without the feathery tops that would develop as they matured.

"Are we going for that walk?" Ettu's tone was brisk, the one she used when she had a job to do and had decided to get on with it.

"Yes, let's go. It will do both of us good."

Merytre barred the door behind us, although not without a wistful sigh. If Ahmose was here to stay with Tall, I would have invited Merytre to come with us, but we could hardly leave him alone and locked away. If someone entered my chambers, he would be trapped.

As we reached the ground level, I spotted Panouk approaching. He would be a rather handsome man if he wasn't so puffed up with his own importance. He seemed to be alone, and for a moment, I debated whether I should say something about our last conversation. He had made it clear that if Amankhau was somehow involved in the matter of the missing women, he didn't want to know about it. His manner in that conversation made me think Panouk himself was not involved, but his reaction had told me I couldn't trust him regardless, not as long as he still trusted Amankhau.

"My lady Kassaya," Panouk said smoothly as we came within speaking distance. He was all professionalism today. If he was still upset about my suggestion that Amankhau had something to hide, he didn't show it. "Allow me to present Lady Hilde."

The woman who stepped out from behind him was so tiny, she had been entirely hidden, even though Panouk was not a large man. She was dark of both hair and eye, and the top of her head was barely as high as my shoulders.

"Well met, my lady," she said, her voice hardly more than a whisper, as she gave me a deep curtsy.

"Oh, no," I said quickly. "You need not do that."

After all, she must be a new Ornament.

"Come, come," Panouk said before Hilde could reply. "I will show you to your chambers. Do excuse us, Lady Kassaya."

He swept past and Hilde scurried after him. I turned to watch them leave and caught her looking back over her shoulder at me.

CHAPTER 10

"A new Ornament, I presume," Ettu said as we made our way out the front doors. "That will please Lady Tiye."

I smiled a greeting at Khaemope and Karpusa, who guarded the front doors during the day. So far, they had seemed quite amenable and not inclined to ask any questions about my comings and goings, or the mysterious blanket-shrouded person who accompanied me on occasion. I wouldn't call them allies, but their lack of diligence was useful.

We started along one of the paths. The sunlight on my arms was unpleasantly warm and I already regretted coming outside.

"Perhaps I should warn her," I said.

"She probably already knows."

"The Ornament, I mean. Hilde."

"Oh." Ettu walked a little further before she spoke again. "You mean to warn her about Lady Tiye's expectations?"

Tiye would, of course, summon the poor woman to clean

her bathing chamber after someone, presumably one of her maids — I couldn't imagine Tiye doing such a thing herself — spilled a full chamber pot over the floor. Hilde would be expected to present herself to Tiye every day at dawn to clean her bathing chamber until such time as another new Ornament arrived to take over the duty.

"She looked rather delicate," I said.

"It would be a good opportunity for you to form an alliance with her," Ettu said. "If you warn her before Lady Tiye summons her, she will be grateful to you."

"I'm not trying to beat Tiye to her. I just want to warn her. I would have appreciated it if someone had warned me when I arrived."

"I wonder why nobody did?" Ettu mused. "After all, every single person here knows what Lady Tiye does whenever a new Ornament arrives. Why does nobody warn them?"

"Because it is Tiye," I said. "And nobody wants to risk angering her."

Despite my own thoughts about warning Hilde, I didn't want to upset Tiye any more than anyone else did. Our friendship might only be tenuous, but she was not a woman I wanted to be on bad terms with. No, I wouldn't warn Hilde. Perhaps I would regret it later, but for now, at least, I would preserve my friendship with Tiye.

Ettu shrugged and didn't seem inclined to comment further. Maybe that meant she disagreed, but I didn't ask. Let her keep her thoughts to herself if that was what she wanted. Marduk knew there was little privacy in this place other than our own thoughts.

We walked on in silence. Hilde's arrival had freed me from thoughts of Ishtar for a few blessed moments, but now my worries returned. My fear for her. Fretting over how much she might have suffered. Her gut-wrenching absence and the things left unsaid between us. The knowledge that sooner or later, I would have to write to my father.

"Oh, look," Ettu said, drawing me from my thoughts. "It is Sutem."

He was still some distance away, but seemed to be headed directly towards us.

"Good morning, Lady Kassaya," he called. "Ettu."

He seemed to peer behind us, likely hoping Merytre would be following me.

"Good morning, Sutem," I said. "A lovely day."

"Indeed, although it is going to be very hot," he replied. "I suggest you make your walk short and return inside as soon as you can."

"We will," I said.

He halted in front of us and seemed to hesitate.

"I'm afraid Merytre remained in my chambers," I said. "She had a task to take care of."

I could hardly tell him she had to stay with Tall.

"I haven't seen her for a few days." Sutem's tone was easy and if he was disappointed at her absence, he hid it well.

"No doubt you will soon enough."

The words came out sharper than I intended and the look that crossed his face told me he noticed. I searched for a way to explain, but he beat me to it.

"I apologise if I have been taking up too much of her time. It is just that…" His voice trailed away and for a moment I didn't think he was going to say anything more. "I care about her," he said at last. "A lot."

I knew Merytre was interested in him, but I had no idea how deep her feelings ran. I hadn't wanted to pry. But Sutem had freely offered this information.

"Does she feel the same for you?" I asked.

His cheeks reddened and I felt a surge of pity for him. I knew what it was like to give myself away by blushing.

"I don't know," he said, to my surprise. "I have asked, but she will not tell me."

"Why ever not?"

Sutem shrugged. "You would have to ask her, my lady."

Before I could reply, he continued.

"I was very sorry to hear about Lady Ishtar," he said.

The shock of hearing her name hit me hard. My throat felt tight and I swallowed, hoping I could reply without bursting into tears.

"Thank you." It was as much as I could manage.

Ettu must have noticed my distress.

"Marduk, it is already hot out here," she said. "I can feel the sweat running down my neck. Surely the change of season must be almost here. I am dearly looking forward to some cooler weather."

"Indeed." I was relieved to have a reason to leave without looking like I tried to avoid further conversation with Sutem. "We should go back inside."

"Would you…" Sutem's voice trailed away. "Never mind."

"Did you want me to pass on a message for you?" I asked.

"It wouldn't be appropriate for me to ask such a thing of you," he said.

"I would be happy to tell her whatever it is," I said.

"Then would you… would you just tell her I hope to see her again soon?"

"Of course," I said.

We made our farewells, then Ettu and I turned back to the Palace. The breeze had dropped, taking with it any pleasantness, and the air was still and hot.

"The sweat is making my gown stick to my back," Ettu said.

"Why do you think Merytre won't tell Sutem how she feels about him?" I asked.

Ettu didn't reply, but her face suggested she knew something.

"She has talked with you about it." Hurt prickled, sharp and sudden, but Merytre was my maid. I could hardly expect her to discuss her feelings with me. After all, I had never— I cut myself off, but my surprise at what I had almost thought drew me to an abrupt halt. Ettu walked another couple of paces before realising I had stopped.

"My lady?" she asked, turning back to me. "Is something wrong?"

I could only stare at her, too shocked at myself to formulate a reply. She came to take my arm.

"Are you feeling faint?" she asked. "You have gone very pale. Should I call Sutem to help you inside?"

I shook my head, but still couldn't find any words.

"Do you need to lean on me?" she asked.

"No, no, I am fine," I managed.

We set off again. Now I was able to move, I walked briskly, pretending I could outpace my own thoughts. I couldn't tell Ettu what had stopped me was the realisation that I had never discussed my feelings for Khaemmalu with her.

I had fallen in love with him and I never even realised.

CHAPTER 11

Ettu didn't speak as we made our way back up to my chambers, although I caught her giving me a sideways glance from time to time. Merytre was quick to let us in when Ettu knocked. She slid the bar into place, then went to unlock Tall's door. Ahmose had returned while we were gone and sat in her usual chair, her face sombre.

"Did you have a pleasant walk?" Merytre asked as she came back with Tall at her heels.

Tall went straight to the window, standing to the side as he always did, so nobody would see him if they happened to look this far up. Merytre hesitated, and I guessed she wanted to join him to look for Sutem, but she gave a little sigh and sat on the couch. She smoothed her skirt over her knees and looked enquiringly at me.

"It was very warm," I said. "We didn't walk for long."

Ettu fanned her face with her hand to demonstrate the truth of my words. Merytre pursed her lips, as if stopping herself from asking after Sutem.

"We saw Sutem," I said. "He said to tell you he hopes to see you again soon."

"Oh." Merytre's cheeks coloured and she raised one hand to her wig, smoothing her hair.

"You may go for a walk if you wish," I said.

"You did say it is rather hot out there," she said. "Perhaps I will wait until later when it is cooler."

Maybe she didn't want to look too eager. I restrained myself from telling her what Sutem said about not knowing how she felt. Ettu would probably tell her anyway, and it was clear Merytre didn't want to confide in me. I didn't want to look like I was pushing her.

Ahmose caught my eye and the expression on her face made my heart skip. She gave me a slight nod and touched one finger to her lips, as if signalling she needed to speak with me privately.

"Why don't you go now?" I said to Merytre. "Take Ettu with you."

"Oh, but—" Ettu started.

Merytre shook her head, but I raised my hand to forestall any argument.

"Go," I said. "I would much rather you go now than spend the day moping about it."

"It is awfully hot," Ettu said. "Perhaps we could wait until late afternoon when the sun is not quite so fierce."

I fluttered my fingers towards the door and tried to pretend I didn't feel bad about sending them out into the heat.

"Go on," I said.

They left without further protest, although I didn't miss the reproachful look Ettu gave me. She, at least, guessed I was sending them away for some reason other than Merytre's obvious desire to see Sutem. As the door closed behind them, Ahmose groaned and started to get to her feet.

"Sit," I said. "I will get it."

It was only as I went to bar the door that I remembered Tall. He was frozen beside the window, a horrified look on his face. He knew we had all forgotten him. He caught my eye and gave me a sorrowful gaze, then hurried out. The door to his bedchamber closed softly.

My cheeks burned. We had hurt him at a time when he already felt bad enough. He had not yet emerged from the melancholy that seemed to have overtaken him since he and Half fled Pharaoh's palace, and in fact, he seemed to feel even worse now Half had gone back without him. I would apologise to him just as soon as I heard whatever it was Ahmose wanted to tell me. I took my seat on the couch again and nodded at her.

"Go on then," I said.

"Pharaoh's palace has a library," she said. "That is a place where books are stored."

"I know what a library is," I said. "What of it?"

"This particular library contains some very special books." She gave me a look that seemed loaded with significance. "Powerful books."

"Books of magic?"

"Books that contain every spell known to my people."

I squashed down the doubt that arose within me. Surely there must be a great many spells. Was it possible for any library to contain them all?

"How did you learn this?" I asked.

"I asked some questions. Very discreetly, of course."

"Who of?"

She shook her head. "Someone I can trust. It is better if I

don't tell you her name. If this all comes out somehow, you know only that I claimed to have learned about some spell books, but not where my knowledge came from."

Although I wanted to know all the details, I had to concede her reasoning was sound. Amankhau had threatened Ettu with torture to get a confession out of her. What would he do to me if he thought I possessed illicit knowledge? He clearly disliked me, so he would be quick to treat me harshly. I couldn't be tortured to provide information I didn't have. Or, rather, I could be tortured, but I wouldn't be able to tell him anything. I prayed to Marduk it would never come to that.

"So Pharaoh's library contains scrolls of spells," I said. "Go on."

"You seek spells of a certain type." She seemed to carefully avoid saying I wanted a spell to make me powerful enough that even Pharaoh would fear me. "If such a spell exists, I believe it will be in this library."

"So you need access to his books."

She gave me a steady look. "Yes."

"How do you propose to gain that?"

"That, Princess, is where the danger lies. There are several options, none of which are without risk. I can take the invisibility potion and search the library myself."

"You have none of the herb you need. The special one."

She had used the last of that herb for the two doses for Half.

"True," she said. "I would need to obtain more, and the risk of discovery is still high even if I could get into the library."

After all, her potion only worked against whoever the user thought of as they drank it. It wouldn't be effective against anyone else who happened to enter the library while she was there.

"What are the other options?" I asked.

"We could ask someone to search the library for us."

"Who? Nobody I know would have that sort of access, and even if they did, how could we be sure it was safe to tell them what we seek?"

"The spell books are in a special collection which is kept in a locked chamber within the very centre of the library." Ahmose gave me a significant look. "Only two librarians have access to this chamber — men by the names of Messui and Shotmaadje."

"I don't know of either of them," I said. "I have never even heard their names before."

"My informant believes they can be bribed."

Everything around us faded away as I finally comprehended the danger of this plan. There was no loyalty amongst bribed men. If someone offered a better bribe, they could turn on me in an instant. Execution would probably seem like a favourable fate compared to whatever punishment might be given to someone caught bribing the royal librarians for access to forbidden spells.

If my goal was to make myself powerful enough for Pharaoh to fear me, I needed more power than a god.

It was far more than mere treason to pursue such a thing.

This was heresy.

CHAPTER 12

"What kind of bribe would the librarians require?" I asked Ahmose, trying to look as calm and unbothered as she did.

"Something expensive," she said. "It would have to be valuable enough to make it worth their while to not only provide the information we seek, but also to hold their silence about it."

"I have the sapphire from Pharaoh."

"He has not yet seen you wearing it," she said. "Is there something else you could offer?"

"The jewel he gave Ishtar then."

Satisfaction oozed through me at the thought of that particular gem being the one that would bribe a man to give us the information we needed to work against Pharaoh.

Ahmose nodded. "It is more valuable than any jewel most men would ever possess."

"How would we do this?" I asked. "How do we make contact with these librarians?"

"My contact knows Messui. She could speak with him on your behalf."

"Absolutely not. We can't involve anyone else."

It was one thing for Ahmose to discretely ask a few questions, but another entirely for her to ask this person, whoever it was, to offer a bribe for me.

"We can trust her," Ahmose said. "I trust her."

"Would you trust her with your life, though?" Would you trust her with *my* life was what I really meant. "And do you trust this Messui not to turn her in?"

She looked me right in the eyes and nodded.

"I trust her," she said.

What other option did I have? There must be very few people who knew the kind of spell that would make me powerful enough to hold a god accountable for his actions. In order to obtain such power, at some point someone other than Ahmose would have to know what I sought. I took a deep breath and hoped that if this was a bad decision, I would live to regret it.

"Very well." If Ahmose thought we could trust her contact, that had to be enough. Her counsel was always wise and she had never given me any reason to doubt her. "I will go get the gem for you."

In my bedchamber, I took Ishtar's gem from the small crate that held what was left of the items I brought with me from Babylon. It didn't really belong in this crate, which contained the last of my most treasured possessions, but I put it there with the knowledge that if I myself had reason to flee urgently, this crate would be the one thing I would be sure to take with me. The rest of Ishtar's jewels were still in the box we took from her chambers.

There wasn't much left in my little crate. The shawl Ishtar made for me had gone to Gautseshen to thank her for stitching Half back together. It was no more than a bitter-sweet memory now. I would have liked to still have the shawl — something tangible to remember my sister by — but how could I regret giving it up when it had gone to the woman who saved my friend's life?

My hairbrush with the handle made from the tusks of a creature that was supposedly as big as a temple went to Tiye for obtaining the location of Abar's sister. All that remained in the little chest now was the shell Father brought me from Syria and a few jewels, including my favourite, a yellow gem cut into the shape of a heart. I remembered it glistening like sunlight the day my father gave it to me. It was dull now, perhaps in need of cleaning. The wooden heart-shaped setting still held it snugly, but there was a crack through the back that I didn't remember. This had always been one of my most trea-sured possessions and it pleased me it wasn't this jewel I had to give up today.

Something moved within my belly. Just the faintest flutter, barely noticeable. The babe? If it was, it would be the first time I had felt him move. I set my hand on my belly and held myself very still, hardly daring even to breathe, as I waited for the feeling again. But if it had indeed been my babe, he was still now.

His small movement reminded me of a conversation I had almost forgotten. I told Ahmose I wanted to be queen in order to be near my child as he grew up. Then Ishtar disappeared and Khaemmalu told me Pharaoh sometimes mistreated his women. My grief and the burning need for justice for Ishtar had overtaken everything else. But would making myself into someone Pharaoh feared mean I forsook any chance to watch my son grow up? I didn't need to be told of the consequences if my efforts were uncovered. Death was the only possibility.

I would have little contact with my babe once he was born. As a son of Pharaoh, he would live in Pharaoh's own palace, but I could expect to receive letters from him when he was old enough, and I would surely see him from time to time. But if I was caught, I would be executed, and I didn't know whether my punishment might also be extended to my son. If he was the most important thing to me, as surely he should be, I would forget about trying to bring Pharaoh to justice. I would accept I couldn't change this world I found myself in, however wrong it was.

I wrapped my fingers around the little heart, still warring with myself. It seemed my choices came down to my son or my sister. The certainty of life with one of them, or the possibility of vengeance for the other. Were they my only options? Was there no way I could achieve both?

But Ishtar was gone and so was any chance I might have had to save her. My son had his whole life ahead of him. If I lived, there would be time to make it up to him for not putting him first before he was even born. There was no other way to atone to Ishtar.

Please Marduk, let my son live. If this all goes wrong, don't let my actions mean he has no chance at life.

I returned the yellow gem to the crate and studied Ishtar's sapphire. My fingers closed around it as I made a silent promise, although I couldn't have said whether it was to Ishtar, or my son, or even to Pharaoh.

Farewell, I thought. *I have to trust you will serve me well.*

Back in the sitting chamber, I pressed the gem into Ahmose's hand.

"Be careful," I said to her.

She nodded and the gem disappeared into her pouch.

"I will, my lady," she said. "I believe this will get the information you seek."

CHAPTER 13

As I sat on the stool in my bathing chamber the following morning, I let my mind drift. I hadn't slept well last night, which had become a regular occurrence. Half-remembered dreams of lions and flowers still lingered. I paid no attention to the maids' conversation until someone nudged me. Ettu presumably.

"I have heard she's very beautiful," one of my maids was saying. I couldn't pick her voice. Hemetre maybe, or Khensa. I still had trouble telling the two of them apart.

"Is she Egyptian?" someone else asked. Ipu, I thought.

"From Britannia," the first woman confirmed. "Apparently her father wants Pharaoh to—"

"Whatever her father wants," Ettu said firmly. "It is none of our concern. She is an Ornament and we should give her the same respect we give any Ornament."

"We are not disrespecting her," someone said. I had given up trying to put names to the voices. "We are only curious."

"Perhaps curiosity would best be entertained in the

privacy of your dormitories," Sehener said as I opened my eyes.

She was the only one I could always identify since her narrow face was so distinctive. Her and Abar. With the others I wasn't always certain I knew which was which.

"I'm sure Lady Tiye will be pleased," someone said, her voice sly. Whoever it was, she was out of my line of sight.

"Enough, Tuya," Ettu said firmly.

It was obviously Hilde they discussed. Even though she had only arrived last night, the women obviously already expected Tiye to summon her. It had been Ishtar who cleaned Tiye's bathing chamber most recently, right up until the day she disappeared. My heart ached and I quickly pushed the thought away.

"Oh, and did you hear about—" someone started, but she was quickly shushed by the others.

I wondered if she had been about to mention the gossip about me being responsible for my sister's disappearance. I had actually wondered why none of my maids had asked about it. After all, they were supposedly eager to correct any mistruths about me. Maybe Ettu had told them I didn't want them to do so. Still, I was somewhat surprised they never asked.

Once my maids finally left, I decided to go for a walk. I wanted to avoid Tiye's chambers today, lest I encounter Hilde. Like me, she would surely wonder why nobody warned her about Tiye's special task for new Ornaments. I had the perfect opportunity and I hadn't done so. She would surely know that was deliberate. I wasn't even certain it was the right decision.

Both Ettu and Merytre decided to accompany me on my walk, with Merytre, in particular, being especially keen. I chose a path that made a circuitous route around the gardens.

The path wasn't wide enough for three, so Merytre dropped back to walk behind us. From the corner of my eye I saw Ettu tipping her face up to the sunlight. I wished I could do the same, but she was more sure-footed than me. I'd fall over my own feet if I tried while we were walking.

A figure approached us from the direction of the wall. He had probably been making a circuit of the perimeter before he spotted us.

"Sutem," Merytre said as he reached us. Her voice was warm and she made no attempt to hide her pleasure at encountering him.

He gave her an easy smile, then turned to me with a little bow.

"My lady," he said. "May I accompany you for a while?"

"Of course," I answered. "But there is only room on the path for Ettu and I to walk together, so you'll need to walk with Merytre."

"That will be quite fine," he said with something that might have been a wink. It happened so fast, I wasn't sure whether I imagined it. Maybe he just had something in his eye.

We set off again and when I looked back next, Merytre and Sutem dawdled some distance behind us.

"He is just as entranced with her as she is with him," Ettu said quietly.

"It is lovely she has found someone she cares for here. This is not a place that..."

My voice trailed away. I had never expected to marry for love, so why was I thinking so wistfully about how this wasn't a place where one might expect to find someone to care about? I had always known, right from when I was a little girl, that my father would determine my fate. That as a woman, I could have no expectation of deciding for myself what I wanted from my life. The best I could have expected was that, with time, I would grow to love the man my father chose for me.

I pushed Khaemmalu's face from my mind and hoped Ettu didn't notice my blush. Why was I even thinking about him? There could never be anything between us, despite my burgeoning awareness of my feelings for him.

From the sideways look Ettu gave me, I knew she hadn't missed the redness in my cheeks. For once, though, she didn't comment.

"Is that Lady Gilukhipa?" she asked instead, with a nod in the direction of a figure heading towards us.

"It could be," I said.

The sun was low in the sky and I couldn't make out much more than a shadow in front of it. It wasn't until we drew closer that I saw it was indeed the Mitanni princess, Gilukhipa. I hadn't spoken to her since Henutmire's gathering, although we both attended Kia's farewell ceremony.

"Kassaya," Gilukhipa called. "I was hoping to encounter you today."

I didn't answer until we were much closer, not wanting to shout across the grounds. As we met, Gilukhipa turned to walk back in the direction we were headed. Ettu and her maid greeted each other and followed us, walking side by side. When I glanced back, Merytre and Sutem were nowhere in sight. I restrained a smile. Let her have her fun. As a servant, there were no restrictions on who could touch her.

"I heard about your sister," Gilukhipa said. "That she chose to return home."

Her voice gave no indication of whether she believed her own words, and when I glanced at her, she was looking off to the side. I couldn't see her face well enough to read it.

"Do you really believe that?" I kept my voice low. Even though I couldn't see anyone close enough to hear us other than Ettu and Gilukhipa's own maid, I'd been here long enough to know there was always a guard lurking in the shadows.

"I suppose it doesn't matter what I believe, does it?" Gilukhipa's gaze was firmly focussed on a nearby garden bed. "The administrators have said she went home."

I swallowed the hasty retort that threatened to burst from me. Of course the administrators would say that. Panouk said it right to my face when I demanded he send people out to search for Ishtar. It was what they said every time a woman disappeared, and surely nobody here believed it any more than I did.

"There was talk she might edge Tiye out of the Top position," I said. "Would any woman who thought she had a chance at becoming Pharaoh's Favourite just walk away?"

"Hush." She shot me the briefest of looks, before turning her attention to the garden bed again. "You shouldn't say such things."

"She couldn't go home. Our father wouldn't take her back. He sent her here and he expected her to stay here."

"Kassaya." Gilukhipa's tone held a warning. "No good can come of questioning the administrators."

"They need to be questioned. Too many women have disappeared and the administrators always say the same thing: she went home. Just like they did when Nebtu disappeared. They always leave in the dead of night and without farewelling a single person they were close to. I know nobody believes it, so why does everyone pretend they do?"

We walked a little way in silence and after a bit, I assumed

Gilukhipa wasn't going to answer me. But it seemed she was just trying to find the right words.

"We have no choice," she said at last. "Kassaya, this can be an easy place to live, but you seem determined to make trouble for yourself."

"How is trying to find my sister making trouble? Someone knows what has happened to her."

"If she has disappeared, there is nothing you can do to help her."

"What if I had evidence about what happened to her?"

Half would surely return soon, and would hopefully bring enough information to satisfy anyone who might still believe the administrators. Gilukhipa shot me a look and I couldn't miss the fear in her eyes. She shook her head.

"The best advice I can give you, Kassaya, is that you should keep your mouth shut," she said. "Even if you think you know what happened to your sister."

She abruptly turned and strode off in the other direction. Her maid hurried after her and Ettu caught up to me again.

"Lady Gilukhipa left in a hurry," she said. The curiosity in her voice suggested she had heard nothing of our conversation.

"We were talking about Ishtar. She said I should keep my mouth shut, even if I have evidence about what happened to her."

"You have been told something like that a number of times now," Ettu observed.

"I think some folk know far more than they are saying. I just don't understand why they all pretend they don't."

If I had pieced together enough information to know Pharaoh was responsible in the short time I had been here, surely others had too.

"Perhaps they suspect, but have no evidence," Ettu said.

From the corner of my eye, I caught movement as Merytre and Sutem emerged from behind some bushes. She hurried towards us, straightening her gown as she did. Sutem gave me a friendly wave and disappeared back into the shadows.

"Your wig is crooked," Ettu observed as Merytre reached us.

"Oh my." Merytre quickly straightened it, avoiding looking at either of us as she did. "I don't know how that happened. It must have been the wind."

We set off again, following the path as it wound back around towards the Palace.

"By the way, Merytre," Ettu said over her shoulder as we walked. "The wind also left grass on your cheek."

CHAPTER 14

"Good morning," I said to Henutmire as I took my usual place beside her in the dining chamber a couple of days later.

I had gone to break my fast a little later than usual and hadn't expected to find her still here. The dining chamber was crowded, mostly with Ornaments whose faces I recognised by now, even if I didn't know their names. Henutmire greeted me with a nod. The serving women brought their platters for me to choose from and it was only after they left that she leaned closer.

"Is there any news on Ishtar?" she asked in a low voice.

Unlike Gilukhipa, Henutmire seemed willing to admit she didn't believe the administrators' claims that each missing woman chose to leave. She certainly hadn't believed them when Nebtu disappeared.

"Nothing." My cheeks reddened with my lie and I sipped my goat's milk, hoping she wouldn't notice. I could hardly tell her what we suspected while we sat here in the dining chamber, surrounded by so many other women.

Henutmire gave me an assessing look. She knew I was lying, or she at least suspected. But what could I tell her that wouldn't raise more questions? If I said we had confirmed Ishtar arrived at Pharaoh's palace the night she disappeared, Henutmire would ask how we knew, and I didn't think Tiye would thank me for revealing she had a way of obtaining such information. I couldn't tell her one of Pharaoh's personal guards said Ishtar reached Pharaoh himself that night. And I definitely couldn't tell her that even now Half was in Pharaoh's palace searching for an answer.

"I have contacts who are doing what they can," I said, hoping she would take this much information as an apology for what I couldn't tell her. We had become friends of sorts, and so much as I could trust anyone here, I did trust Henutmire. But the secrets I kept didn't affect only me. "So far, though, they have not uncovered anything definite."

Henutmire sighed and shook her head.

"I'm so sorry." Her voice was warm and she sounded genuinely regretful. "I understand how hard it is to not know."

"Henutmire." I paused, debating with myself whether I should even ask. Henutmire had been the only person who was willing to admit she didn't believe Nebtu had merely left. Hopefully she would be more receptive to my question than Tiye, who told me there was nothing Pharaoh could do to me that anyone would criticise him for. I checked to make sure none of the serving women were within earshot before I whispered to her. "Has Pharaoh ever hurt you?"

Henutmire stiffened and her gaze darted around the chamber as if she checked for any sign someone had heard me.

"Shush," she said. "You mustn't speak of things like that."

"You know you can trust me. I have proven it."

Indeed, I had arranged for her letter to Nebtu's family to be smuggled out of the Palace. She knew I had used some illicit means, even if she didn't know the details. The scribe, Pentau, would never have sent such a letter for her.

Henutmire fumbled as she reached for her mug. The mug tipped over and melon juice spilled out.

"Oh my." Henutmire jumped up, her lap already soaked with the pink liquid.

Serving women rushed to clean the mess, efficiently wiping down her table and replacing her crockery. Henutmire's maid, who had been standing against the wall with Ettu, hurried over with a towel.

"How clumsy of me," Henutmire said as her maid dabbed ineffectually at the pink stain on her skirt.

"Can I do anything to help?" I asked.

"No, no, the servants have it cleaned up already. Oh my, what a mess I made. I need to go change."

She hurried out of the chamber without looking at me again. Her hand had shook as she reached for the mug, but was it really an accident? It was certainly an efficient way to shut down a conversation she didn't want to have.

"What happened with Lady Henutmire?" Ettu asked as we walked back to my chambers a little later.

"I asked her—" I stopped as a messenger boy raced past, then continued in a whisper. "I asked if Pharaoh had ever hurt her. And she… panicked, I suppose. She said I shouldn't ask, then she knocked over her mug."

"On purpose?"

"I'm not sure."

We turned down the last hallway, the one that led only to Tiye's and my suites.

"Maybe she knew what I was talking about, but hasn't

experienced it herself," I said. "She has only lain with Pharaoh twice, so maybe he hasn't…"

"Had the opportunity yet," Ettu finished. "She may know of another woman who has been hurt."

"If I had to guess, I would say it's someone she knows personally, not just gossip she heard."

Nebtu, perhaps. Did Henutmire know more about her friend's disappearance than she had revealed?

"I think a lot of the women here know more than they say," Ettu said. "And not just the Ornaments. Their maids would know too. After all, they're the ones who tend to their mistresses when they return with bruises. Even if their mistresses refuse to talk about what happened, a woman doesn't need to be terribly clever to put it together."

Back in my chambers, Ahmose sat at a little table. Two other chairs were drawn up to it, presumably for Merytre and Tall. On the table lay a rectangular box marked with a grid and scattered with playing pieces. I had seen a box like that in Tiye's chambers recently. Merytre unlocked Tall's door and they both returned to the table.

"What are you doing?" I asked, going over to inspect the box.

"Teaching Tall to play *senet*," Merytre said. "Have you ever played?"

"No, but I think Tiye does," I said.

"It's a game of strategy," Ettu said, coming to stand between Merytre and Ahmose's chairs. "A couple of the maids were talking about it. I have never played either, but I would like to learn."

We watched as Ahmose rolled the dice and moved a playing piece.

"I can teach you," Merytre said. I wasn't sure whether she

meant me or Ettu. "It's fun, although Ahmose and Tall are taking it a lot more seriously than I do."

Indeed, Tall had barely waited until Ahmose finished her turn before he snatched up the dice and rolled. He studied the grid with a frown, his hand hovering over a playing piece.

"Are you sure?" Ahmose asked him. "Remember your goal. Think about what I will do next if you move that particular piece."

Tall groaned and moved his hand back. After a few moments of contemplation, he reached for a different playing piece. He glanced at Ahmose, as if waiting for her to comment, but when she said nothing, he moved his piece.

"A good decision," Ahmose said, swiftly moving one of her own pieces. "And see how you blocked me there. It will take me another couple of moves to get past you now."

Tall flashed her a grin and moved his next piece with more confidence.

"Win!" he said.

"Not this time, I'm afraid." Ahmose moved another piece and Tall let out a groan.

I returned to the dining chamber the following morning, even though it wasn't usual for me to eat there two days in a row. I wanted to ask Henutmire again whether Pharaoh had ever hurt her and I hoped she might be more willing to tell me since my question wouldn't come as quite so much of a surprise this time.

There were women here who knew about what Pharaoh did, and maybe they even knew why. If I could learn that, I might be able to piece together exactly what had happened to Ishtar. But Henutmire wasn't there when I arrived, and although I dallied long past when I would normally leave, she never came.

"I will go back tomorrow," I said to Ettu as we returned to my chambers. "And every day until she tells me."

"Are you sure that is wise?" she asked. "Right now, Lady Henutmire is an ally. If she won't tell you, it's because she is afraid."

She was right, as usual. Henutmire wasn't withholding whatever she knew to prevent me from uncovering the truth about what happened to Ishtar. She was afraid, and if I continued to push her, I would only drive her away.

There were so many women here, but so few I could trust. I couldn't be certain who else I could ask that wouldn't immediately report me to the administrators. There were surely other Ornaments who would keep my secret, but I couldn't afford to ask the wrong one. And even if I sent Merytre, who had lived at the Palace her whole life, to ask around amongst the servants, what if she asked the wrong person and they reported her to the administrators?

"I don't like to say this." Ettu shot me a look as if trying to gauge how I might respond. "But maybe it is time to stop asking questions. You will draw attention to yourself."

"But if I don't ask, who will? The more we learn, the clearer it becomes that many people here at least suspect the truth about what happens to the women who disappear, but nobody is willing to do anything about it."

"Because they can't," Ettu said with a shrug. "You know that. He is above the law."

"There must be a way to hold him accountable. I can't believe the gods would want such a travesty to continue."

"The people here believe him to be a god."

We reached the door to my chambers and she raised her hand to knock, but paused to study me.

"My lady, I know it is a terrible thing and you grieve for

Lady Ishtar. We all do. But I worry you will draw too much attention to yourself."

"And what would be the consequence of that?"

My voice was tarter than I intended. I thought she understood how important it was to reveal the truth about not just Ishtar, but all the missing women.

"I don't know," she said with a shrug. "But we also don't know who we can trust. We suspect this conspiracy reaches very high levels within two palaces. It would only take one person who is involved to hear you're asking questions they would rather you didn't. They might decide you need to be silenced."

"If I disappear, you must tell everyone what we have learned. Every Ornament, every servant. Write to my father, but not through Pentau. Write to my mother as well. Tell every single person you can find."

"And that would make targets of all of us."

She knocked on the door, effectively cutting off our conversation.

CHAPTER 15

Henutmire was in her usual seat in the dining chamber the following morning. She didn't look up as I settled myself at the next table.

"Good morning, Henutmire," I said.

She gave me a too-brief smile and quickly bit into some bread. I figured she was making sure she couldn't speak to me. I waited until the serving women had left, then leaned over to whisper to her.

"I wanted to remind you I got that letter to Nebtu's family out of the Palace," I said. "And nobody other than myself and my servants know about it."

Henutmire chewed for a little longer, then swallowed.

"Are you trying to blackmail me?" Her voice was cold.

"Of course not. It was a reminder you can trust me."

She fiddled with her bread and didn't meet my eyes. I waited, restraining myself from saying anything else only with great effort.

"I know that," she said at last. "Please believe me, Kassaya.

If I don't answer your questions, it's not because I don't trust you."

"I didn't mean to upset you," I said. "I just don't understand why nobody will talk about it."

Her gaze darted up to meet mine, then flicked away. She gave a heavy sigh as she shredded her bread and scattered the pieces on the plate.

"Kassaya, you have been here long enough to understand how things work," she said.

"Tell me how they work then," I said. "Because I obviously don't understand."

But Henutmire shook her head and took another bite, clearly signalling the end of the conversation.

"Please," I whispered to her. "You know my sister is missing, and we still don't know what happened to Nebtu. I'm just trying to figure it out. If you know something that could help, please tell me."

But Henutmire resolutely took another bite and gave no sign she had heard me. I let the matter drop. Pushing her wouldn't help. I would be more likely to get something out of her by letting her reveal what she knew in her own time.

As we walked back to my chambers a little later, I told Ettu about my conversation with Henutmire.

"Why do they keep his secret?" I asked. "Ishtar told me Pharaoh hurt her, but only because I saw the bruises. Tiye wouldn't tell me anything, and neither would Henutmire. Even Gilukhipa obviously knows something."

We passed two servants who had stopped to chat.

"That's her," I heard one of them say as we passed. "The one I told you about."

My cheeks heated and I stopped myself from looking back

at them. Maybe they weren't even talking about me. They could have meant Ettu since her manner of dress was so unusual. But they could also have been talking about how some folk thought I was responsible for Ishtar's disappearance. I straightened my back and kept walking. I would not disgrace myself by going back to demand they say whether it was me they spoke of. Ettu seemed to shoot me a sideways look and I guessed she had heard them too.

"If nobody is willing to talk, then we can only speculate," she said. "I expect they are afraid."

"But of what?"

"That they will be the next to go missing, I suppose."

Absently, I noted the Eye of Horus hanging from a cord around the neck of a servant woman who came down the hallway towards us. She didn't acknowledge us as she passed, too intent on whatever her task was. My own amulet — a gift from Neferu — was safely in the pouch at my waist. I hadn't looked at it since I put it in there. I couldn't bear to. It made me feel too odd.

"But how would that happen unless I reveal what they tell me?" I asked once the servant woman was far enough away. "And not to just anyone. I would have to tell someone who is involved with whatever is going on."

"They don't know whether they can trust you," she said with a shrug. "Just as you aren't sure who you can trust either. You have been here for less than a season. It's not long enough for anyone to really get to know you."

"But I have done nothing to show them they can't trust me."

But I had, hadn't I? I kept asking questions when they warned me not to. We turned down the hallway that led to my chambers.

"Oh," Ettu said. "Is that Belet-ili?"

It was indeed Belet-ili slumped against the wall opposite my door. I wondered whether she had knocked and Merytre told her to wait outside, or whether she knew I wasn't there and had decided to wait for me. Hopefully Merytre knew she was here and Tall was safely locked away in the men's bedchamber. I couldn't risk taking Belet-ili inside, though, without knowing. Whatever she wanted would have to be said out here in the hallway.

Belet-ili peeled herself off the wall when she saw us. As we drew closer, I could see her eyes were swollen and red.

"Belet-ili," I said. "What brings you here?"

"My lady, I have been told I am to be reassigned." Her voice wobbled and her eyes shone with tears. "Since Lady Ishtar has left, both her chambers and her lady's maids have been allocated to someone else."

It hurt to hear her say Ishtar had left, although I knew it wasn't what she believed. It was she who had come to tell me Ishtar hadn't returned from Pharaoh's palace. Had Hilde inherited both Ishtar's chambers and her maids? She was the only new Ornament I knew of. Perhaps she didn't want Belet-ili.

"I see," I said, feeling like I needed to say something, but not knowing what response was appropriate.

I knew what she wanted from me, but I couldn't help her. She was too close to Nammu and I couldn't trust either woman. Belet-ili waited, perhaps expecting me to offer.

"Will you allow me to serve you again?" she asked when I only looked at her. "I can't bear to be assigned to a stranger."

I considered my words carefully before I spoke. I didn't want to give her a reason to cause problems for me. Nammu had already done enough of that when she tried to frame me for the theft of Tiye's jewels.

"I'm afraid I already have a full contingent of maids," I said, hoping my tone conveyed regret. "Perhaps if one of them was to be reassigned, I might be able to consider you, but right now…"

I let my voice trail away as I shrugged. Belet-ili's eyes narrowed. She obviously hadn't expected me to refuse her.

"I travelled with you from Babylon." Her voice was haughty now. "Even though I had no wish to."

"You forget I had no wish to come here either."

"You could have persuaded your father," she said. "I had no choice."

I only shook my head. There was no point arguing with her about it. Nammu said Ishtar had told her I asked for her three maids to be sent to Egypt with me. It was a lie, but I never had the chance to ask Ishtar whether she really said it.

"You owe me this," Belet-ili said. "I am your responsibility since you brought me here."

It wouldn't matter what I said. Belet-ili had obviously decided she was entitled to come back to me, but I had Tall's safety to consider. There was already enough risk to him without the complication of a woman whose loyalty I was unsure of. It might be fine to start with, but what would Belet-ili do the first time she was upset about something? Would she seek revenge by reporting Tall's presence? Would she hint to Nammu that she knew something the other woman didn't? Nammu would take any opportunity to ruin me and a few veiled suggestions from Belet-ili might be enough for her to go to the administrators.

"I cannot take you," I said. "And that is my final word on the matter."

Belet-ili glared at me for long enough that I wondered what I would do if she refused to leave. I supposed I could call for Panouk to intervene, but he might well decide to reassign her back to me and how would I get out of it then?

But to my surprise, Belet-ili chose not to argue any further. With one last glare, she sniffed disdainfully, then strode away.

CHAPTER 16

Shortly after Belet-ili left, a knock came at the door. I sighed, expecting it to be her again, come back with a new argument for why I should take her back into my service. But it was a messenger boy with an invitation for me to dine with Pharaoh the following evening. Ettu accepted before I could object. I could hardly refuse anyway. But knowing I would see him so soon left me sleepless that night.

It would be the first time I had seen Pharaoh since Ishtar disappeared. The first time since I had learned he was probably responsible for her disappearance. For her murder. I hoped I could look at him without revealing my anger and hatred and desire for vengeance.

I was also afraid. Without knowing the circumstances of what happened between him and my sister, I didn't know how much I should fear for my own safety.

"My lady, you are very tense," Ettu said as my maids prepared me for the dinner. "It is quite obvious something is wrong to anyone who cares to look."

Her quiet voice was lost in the women's clamour as

they disagreed about which wig I should wear, and whether silver or gold bands on my wrists would look best with my new gown. I took a deep breath and tried to appear more relaxed. I loosened my shoulders, for starters. They ached from the way I was holding them anyway.

"That is a little better," she said. "Your face is very pinched, though. Perhaps you could try smiling."

I bared my teeth at her and she gave me a disapproving look.

"I'm sorry," I muttered. "I just don't think I can smile at him."

I hadn't realised anyone else was listening, but of course they were.

"Oh, my lady," Khensa said. "You must not let yourself be intimidated by Pharaoh."

"You are easily the most beautiful of all the Ornaments," Nebetah said.

"Your face has an exotic look that is quite rare," added Hemetre.

"Your skin is so soft," Sehener said.

"And your eyes are magnificent," Ipu said.

Mutnofret and Tuya added their agreements, by which time I was feeling quite uncomfortable with all the compliments. Merytre nodded at everything they said, but at least she didn't add to their blatant flattery. Ettu pursed her lips and I was sure she tried not to smile.

Only Abar didn't seem to be listening. She stood off to one side, holding the finger rings I would wear tonight, and making no effort to involve herself in the conversation. Her gaze kept darting over to the door as if she was trying to decide whether she could slip away without being noticed.

"Abar, pass me those finger rings," Sehener said, and the girl handed them over without comment.

I held out my hands and Sehener slipped the finger rings on.

"This one really doesn't suit your gown," she said with a frown, gesturing for Ettu to look.

"Hmm," Ettu said. "I don't think it's that bad."

"But it is not perfect," Sehener said. "What if we swapped it for that silver one with the flowers engraved on it?"

"The narcissus?" Ettu asked. "Or the lotus?"

"The narcissus," I said before Sehener could reply.

I had dreamed of narcissus. Over and over. They said something important to me and it bothered me that I couldn't remember what it was. If I was to wear a flower, it should be a narcissus.

"Your other finger rings are locked away." Ettu's tone was casual and she kept her gaze on my hand, which I still held out for their inspection. "Do you wish me to fetch the one with the narcissus?"

I knew what she was trying to say. She would have to unlock the door to the men's bedchamber and there was a possibility someone would spot Tall.

"No," I said. "Let's not bother. I won't wear this one, though."

Sehener took the ring off my finger with no more than a nod. I was a little surprised she didn't argue I should wear the one with the narcissus. Did this suggest my maids sensed some oddness about the story that my jewels were locked away to keep them safe and they tried not to draw attention to it?

The women resumed their chatter and I sat in silence as they finished making up my face. After three changes of sandals, they finally pronounced me ready and Ettu handed me the hand mirror. I inspected my face and told them they had done very well. They departed with smiles and good wishes for my evening with Pharaoh, all except for Abar who said nothing and was the first to make her escape out into the hallway.

Once the door was safely closed behind them, Ettu unlocked Tall's door. He yawned as he came out to the sitting chamber. His hair was sticking up and I guessed he must have fallen asleep while he waited for the women to depart. I felt bad he had to spend so long in there every time they attended to me, but there really was no way to hurry them without causing suspicion. After all, most Ornaments adored the daily rituals of being attended to by so many maids.

Ahmose was in her usual chair, her face pensive. If she had spoken to her contact about gaining access to the magic books, she had given me no sign of it. It had been almost a week since our conversation, though, so surely she had made contact with whoever it was by now. Merytre went straight to the window, probably checking to see if Sutem was anywhere within sight, while Ettu dropped onto a couch with a sigh.

"You don't need to leave just yet," she said to me. "There is time to sit for a short while."

I was halfway through lowering myself to a couch when the door to the hallway opened.

It was Sehener.

She took in the sitting chamber in one glance and gasped loudly. Behind her, the door swung open wider.

"Amun," Merytre swore. "I forgot to bar it."

She raced across the chamber to slam the door closed. Sehener seemed to be frozen and barely noticed. Merytre slid the bar into place and stayed there, her hands on the bar as if to make it clear she wouldn't be unlocking the door any time soon.

Sehener's gaze was fixed on Tall. She opened and closed her mouth as if she couldn't figure out what to say.

Tall looked equally horrified. He jumped up and started pacing the length of the chamber, flapping his hands furiously.

Sehener's eyes widened and she looked like she couldn't decide whether to flee or scream. Or perhaps both.

"Sehener, please sit down," Ettu said. "We can explain everything."

Sehener hesitated. She glanced back towards the door as if wondering whether she could leave, but Merytre was there, her hands still holding the bar firmly in place. Sehener's gaze darted from Tall, who still paced and flapped his hands, to me, and back to him.

"Sehener," I said. "Please, let us explain."

Ettu went to take her by the arm and steer her to a chair. Sehener sat abruptly, as if her legs had given out from under her.

"Oh my," she said in a long exhale. "I suspected you were keeping secrets, but never in a million years would I guess it to be something like this. I suppose he is…" Her voice trailed away.

"He is unmodified, if that's what you mean to ask," Ettu said briskly. "And there is a perfectly good explanation for his presence."

Sehener gave herself a little shake and nodded.

"I'm sure there is," she said, sounding as if she tried to match Ettu's no-nonsense tone. "And I would be very happy if someone would tell it to me, but whether you choose to explain or not, you may be assured I will keep your secret."

I had thought we could trust Sehener and it was gratifying to know I was right.

"This is Tall," I said, gesturing towards him. "Tall, please sit down. Sehener is one of my maids. We can trust her."

Tall gave Sehener a look that was as wary as the one she gave him, but he did stop pacing. He returned to his chair, but before he sat, he turned to Sehener and gave her a bow that was surprisingly elegant.

"Lady!" he said.

"Oh." Sehener's cheeks coloured. "Oh, no, I am no lady, only a lady's maid. You need not bow to me."

Tall seated himself, looking much calmer than I would have expected. He had even stopped flapping his hands. Sehener studied him for a moment longer and I wondered what she made of him. He towered above even the tallest of men, but there was still a solidity to him. He was well muscled and strong enough to carry Half all the way from Pharaoh's palace after he was stabbed. His features were pleasant enough, neither particularly handsome nor especially ugly.

Sehener finished her examination of Tall, then turned her attention to me. She gave me a little nod as if to say she was ready to hear my explanation.

"Tall is one of my companions who travelled with me from Babylon," I said. "There is another man who came with us. His name is Half, but he is not here at the moment."

My heart ached with sudden intensity. I had briefly forgotten Ishtar, and that Half had gone to seek information about her fate. How could I have forgotten for even a moment?

"Of course, Tall and Half weren't allowed inside when we arrived," I said. "They went to Pharaoh's palace and lived there until recently when Half was attacked. They had to flee and they came here to us. They have been living in my chambers ever since, although Half has now returned to Pharaoh's palace."

Sehener's face showed her bewilderment and she shook her head as if making no sense of my explanation.

"I don't understand," she said. "How did you get permission for them to be inside?"

"I didn't," I said. "We smuggled them in."

"So the administrators…" she said.

"The administrators do not know," I said.

"Oh my," she breathed. "If they found out—"

"We are aware of the consequences," I said. "Which is why it pleased me to hear your assurance you will not tell anyone."

"Of course not," she said. "My lady, I realise this situation is of the utmost seriousness and although I understand the reasons for your caution, I am also saddened to learn you don't trust me."

"It's not that," I said.

She waved her hand at me. "I understand why you would trust nobody other than those who live here with you. Completely. But I thought you knew you had my loyalty. I'm sure all your lady's maids feel the same way. None of us have ever had a mistress like you. No other Ornament would treat us to a picnic and then not even ask any extra duties of us."

"Thank you." We eyed each other for a few moments and I made a fast decision. Despite what she said, I needed to give her something to ensure her loyalty and I had already considered inviting her to move in. We had needed an extra woman here ever since Ishtar moved to her own chambers. Before she disappeared, of course. "Sehener, would you like to live here in my chambers with us?"

Her mouth widened in a silent exclamation of surprise and

she gazed around the sitting chamber as if she had never seen it before. With its soft rugs, thick curtains, and assortment of comfortable chairs and couches, it was likely much grander than the maids' dormitories. Merytre said they had beds for the maids, and a chest each, but little else. Sehener's gaze roamed over each of us — Tall, who she kept returning to, Ettu, Merytre, Ahmose. Finally, she turned back to me.

"You mean to say I would have my own bedchamber?" she asked.

"You would have to share with someone."

Perhaps I should have discussed this with Ettu and Merytre first. I could hardly ask Ahmose to share, so it would have to be one of them.

"Actually," Merytre said. "My lady, I was trying to find the right time to tell you this."

She paused and swallowed. Her cheeks looked unusually red. I suspected I knew what her news might be, so I held my tongue and tried not to rush her.

"Sutem has asked me to marry him," she said at last. "He has a house only a block from the Palace, so I would be quite near. I would still serve you, of course, and would come at dawn every day. I'm sorry I didn't tell you earlier."

"That is wonderful news," I said. "But why didn't you tell me?"

"Well, because..." she floundered. "With everything that has been happening, I didn't think it right to ask you just now."

"Ask me? Why would I object to you marrying Sutem?"

"I didn't think you would," she said. "Other mistresses might, but I knew you wouldn't. It just didn't seem right with Lady Ishtar and Half and everything..."

Her voice trailed away and she darted a glance at Sehener.

"You need not watch your tongue around me," Sehener said quickly. "And I don't need to be rewarded in order to keep your secrets, my lady. I hope you believe that. I appreciate the invitation to live in your chambers and it would be such an honour, but I know you have only offered it so I will have reason to keep quiet. You need not give me anything. I am loyal to you regardless."

"You probably won't believe me now," I said, "but I was already considering asking you."

Sehener's eyes widened and she raised one hand to cover her mouth.

"It would be useful to have another woman here," I said. "Someone I know I can trust. I have been watching you for some time and thinking about it."

"Oh my." Sehener's hand fluttered back down to her lap and she seemed overcome with emotion. "My lady, I am sure you don't know how much that means to me."

I nodded in acknowledgement and turned back to Merytre.

"Well," I said to her. "It seems congratulations are in order."

"I may marry him?" Merytre asked. "And go to live with him?"

"Of course," I said. "But I don't know the customs here. Is there a contract that needs to be negotiated? A bride price to be paid?"

If Merytre knew who her father was, she had never told me. Her mother was an Ornament, but if Pharaoh had fathered her, surely she would have grown up in his palace, along with all his other sons and daughters.

"Usually a woman's father would negotiate for her," Merytre said. "But Sutem knows I have nobody to speak for me and he doesn't expect any payment."

So perhaps her father was no longer alive. Her mother must have had an affair while she was an Ornament. This didn't seem like an appropriate time to ask.

"I will speak for you," I said. "You can make arrangements with Sutem for us to talk tomorrow."

I had no idea what such a discussion might involve. I supposed I would just tell Sutem he should treat her kindly and provide for her needs. Theirs would be a love match, and that was more than most women could expect.

A twinge of jealousy stirred within me and I pushed it away. I had never expected a love match for myself, a fact I had reminded myself of several times lately. As a princess, I knew from the time I could understand it that my father would select for me a man who was useful to him. I never expected to choose for myself, although I had always hoped it might be a man I would grow to love in time.

"Tall," I said. "Would you fetch one of my jewellery chests? Any one will do."

He got up immediately and hurried out. Sehener's gaze followed him. She looked calmer now and I was pleased to see the look she gave him was more inquisitive than judgemental. Tall returned with a chest and set it down in front of me. He lifted the lid, lay it aside, and gave me a nod, before returning to his chair.

"Merytre, come here," I said.

Her eyes were wide and she kept looking between me and the chest as if she had guessed what I intended, although the look on her face said quite clearly she didn't believe it was happening.

"A marriage gift for you," I said. "Choose an item for yourself. Any one you would like."

"Oh, my lady." Merytre's eyes filled with tears. "I did not

expect such a thing. This is too generous. I'm sure you don't understand the worth of your jewels."

I waved towards the chest.

"Go on," I said. "Whatever you desire."

Merytre peered into the chest. She reached out to tentatively pick up a finger ring, shooting a glance at me as it to check she really had my permission. I nodded encouragingly.

"Take your time," I said. "Don't just choose the first item you see."

Ettu went to the chest and pulled out a necklace, holding it up to Merytre's throat to see how it looked. Emboldened, Merytre let out a little laugh and reached into the chest again. Sehener joined them and soon the three women were immersed in examining various jewels and trying them on Merytre. In just a few minutes, she was draped in necklaces, bracelets, earrings, and finger rings.

My eyes met Ahmose's and she gave me a little nod, as if to say she approved of my actions. My cheeks reddened and I returned my gaze to the three women around the chest. I hadn't been seeking approval. I only wanted to give Merytre a marriage gift since she had nobody else to do such a thing.

CHAPTER 17

*E*ventually, the chatter of the women around my jewellery chest died.

"I would like this one, if I may." Merytre held out her hand to show me the silver finger ring topped with a small emerald chip.

"You wouldn't like something bigger?" I had expected she would choose a larger gem, but Merytre shook her head.

"I have always thought this one to be very pretty," she said. "It is not so extravagant as to draw attention and you never wear it yourself."

"As you wish," I said. "It is yours."

Merytre's smile was broader than I had ever seen on her as she examined the ring on her finger.

"Ettu," I said. "Would you select another item please? This I will give to Sutem as Merytre's bride price."

"Oh," Merytre said with a gasp. "My lady, you have already—"

I waved away her protestation and nodded to Ettu, who reached into the chest. She seemed to know exactly what she was looking for and quickly retrieved another finger ring with a much larger gem. A garnet, perhaps, or a ruby. I couldn't tell the difference, but whatever it was, it was obviously much more valuable than the one Merytre had chosen for herself.

Merytre's eyes were round as Ettu handed me the finger ring. I tucked it away in my pouch with a nod.

"He may trade it or keep it," I said to Merytre. "Go tell him I will speak with him tomorrow morning."

Merytre stammered and didn't seem to be able to find any words. Tall slipped away to the men's bedchamber, taking the chest with him. Ettu barred the sitting chamber door behind Merytre, and turned back to me with a broad grin.

"I'm not sure you quite understand what you have done for her," she said to me. "She told me some time ago she would marry Sutem if he asked, but she was sad she had nobody to negotiate the contract for her."

"I suppose you told her she should negotiate for herself," I said. Ettu had developed some rather strange opinions since she started wearing men's attire.

"Of course I did." She gave me an arch look. "But Merytre is very traditional and wanted things done properly, as she saw it."

Sehener was still standing in the place where the women had gathered around the chest and seemed to be quietly weeping.

"Sehener?" I asked. "Is there a problem?"

Had I done something wrong? Although Ettu obviously approved of my actions, perhaps I had in some way caused offence? The beliefs of the Egyptian people were so strange, it wouldn't surprise me to learn I had done the wrong thing, even if Merytre appeared to be pleased.

"Oh, my lady." Sehener wiped her eyes with her sleeve and gave me a watery smile. "I am merely overcome by everything I have learned today."

Tall returned to settle himself on the couch again. Sehener gestured towards him and seemed to take a few moments to find the right words.

"It is not just your man here," she said at last. "I knew there was some secret being kept, but never imagined it would be something like this. But also—" she motioned towards the door "— what you did for Merytre. I don't know of any other Ornament who would do such a thing for a servant."

"I'm sure plenty would," I said. "We have no idea what happens within the privacy of their own chambers."

"That is true," Sehener said. "So much truer than I realised."

She gave Tall a long look and he studied her in return.

"I am Sehener," she said, giving him a nod. "Well met."

Tall's eyes were wide and he hesitated, presumably searching for the word that would come closest to what he wanted to say, although of course Sehener wouldn't understand that yet. She had seen the way he flapped his hands, but how would she react when she discovered how he spoke?

"Me!" he said.

Sehener waited, studying him with what looked to be curiosity rather than disdain. And it was only now that I realised he had spoken in Egyptian earlier when he called her lady. Although he understood the language well, he had never before been able to utter a word of it. Tall set his hand to his chest and his mouth opened and closed.

"Tall!" he managed finally, once again using Egyptian. "Idiot."

"Tall has trouble finding the right words," I said quickly.

"Some folk say he is an idiot because of that, but here in my chambers we do not think such a thing. He is a friend and a much cherished one at that."

Sehener nodded, a brisk movement that reminded me of the way Ettu might have responded.

"Very well," she said. "Tall, you may be assured I will not think you are an idiot."

As if to prove her words, she went to sit beside him. She smoothed her gown over her knees and looked to me, seemingly waiting for some indication of what was to happen next.

When Merytre returned from seeing Sutem, her eyes were red as if she had been crying. I didn't want to embarrass her by asking why. Surely any tears were of happiness.

"He says he looks forward to speaking with you tomorrow," she said to me. "I can't—"

I guessed what she was about to say and cut her off.

"You have already thanked me," I said. "There is no need to do so again."

"But—" she started.

"Merytre," I said. "I am happy to do it."

Ettu interrupted to point out it was time for me to leave unless I wanted to be late for dinner with Pharaoh. Personally, I cared little about social niceties such as promptness when it came to that man, but it was not worth the argument that would ensue if I said such a thing. Instead, I allowed them to straighten my gown and wig, and inspect my makeup, which, thank Marduk, they decided didn't need to be touched up.

I wore a new gown which had been designed to complement the blue sapphire from Pharaoh. The linen was a pale blue and so tight that I reminded myself to take small steps, fearing the fabric would tear if my strides were too long. The pendant around my throat was heavy, an unwelcome reminder the son I had been thinking of as mine belonged to Pharaoh.

"I don't want to wear this," I said, raising my fingers to touch the sapphire. "Take it off please."

"He will expect to see it on you," Ettu said quickly. "You must wear it at least once."

"It is very fine," Sehener said. "I can't imagine what it would be like to wear such a jewel."

But of course she didn't know what we knew about Pharaoh and this was not the time to explain.

"Get it off me." When nobody moved to help, I fumbled to untie the cord around my neck. "I will not wear it. Not until we know Ishtar's death has been avenged."

The words left my mouth before I realised what I was about to say. I froze, hearing myself. The words rang through my mind. *Ishtar's death. Ishtar's death.* It was the first time I had admitted it out loud.

"Oh, my lady," Sehener murmured. "Such a terrible thing."

I could feel Ettu and Merytre watching me. Waiting for me to tell her what we knew. But I couldn't do it now, right before I saw him. Before I had to dine with him. Spend an evening with him. Perhaps — Marduk, please no — even suffer him to lie with me.

"If somebody doesn't get it off me right now, I will cut it off." I tugged again at the cord. It was like a weight around my neck. A weight that grew heavier with every moment that passed. It would drag me right down into the earth if I wore it long enough.

"Here, let me," Ettu said with a sigh. "I do think you should reconsider, though."

She untied the cord and the relief I felt as my neck was freed was so strong, I would have wept if it wasn't for the knowledge that my eye makeup would run and need to be reapplied before I left.

"I will wear the yellow heart," I said. "It is in my little crate from Babylon."

It had been my favourite ever since Father gave it to me. A reminder of home and family and easier times. Wearing that jewel tonight would give me courage in a way the blue sapphire wouldn't. Ettu went off to fetch the jewel without any further comment.

"Who do you wish to accompany you tonight?" Merytre asked while we waited for Ettu to return. When I glanced at her, her gaze flicked towards Sehener.

"Ettu and Sehener," I said, guessing that was what Merytre intended.

"Oh my," Sehener said with a gasp. "Me?"

"Of course," I said. "All three of you maids will have to take turns to accompany me to such things. Merytre will stay with Ahmose and Tall tonight. We must always have at least one person here with Tall in case someone should try to enter my chambers while I am gone."

Sehener nodded, her eyes still wide.

"Do you have things you need to fetch from your dormitory?" I asked.

"I can get it all tomorrow," she said. "Merytre will want her bed here tonight anyway and I don't have much. I also need to tell one of the administrators so they can reassign my bed if necessary."

"You should see Panouk whenever you must talk to an administrator," I said. "Do not go to Amankhau. He is not to be trusted."

"He makes me feel very uncomfortable," Sehener said with

a nod. "The way he watches us. It is different from how Panouk looks at us. None of the maids like him."

I'd never heard anyone other than Panouk speak positively of Amankhau. My own dislike of him stemmed to the time he said I had made a name for myself as a trouble maker. *Asking too many questions,* he had said. *Poking around in things that are none of your business. Women like you tend to get themselves into trouble.* Nothing he had done since then had changed my opinion of him.

While we were speaking, Ettu had returned with the yellow heart. She fastened it around my neck and studied me with a critical eye.

"It really doesn't go with this gown," she said. "There is no time for you to change, though, and we would have to swap your wig as well. We picked that one because it pairs so beautifully with this gown."

"It is fine," I said. "He won't notice what I wear anyway."

"I pray you are correct," she said with a worried frown.

I met Ahmose's gaze. Her face was as calm as ever, but I sensed her concern.

"Do you have any advice for me?" I asked.

"Be what he expects you to be," she said. "Nothing more and nothing less."

CHAPTER 18

Ifixed my gaze straight ahead as Ettu, Sehener and I made our way along the hallways. I constantly reminded myself to take small steps so as not to tear the delicate fabric.

We passed various Ornaments, servants and runner boys, but I looked at none of them as I prepared myself to face the man who I was almost certain had murdered my sister. For the first time in a long time, I heard the words my mother said to me before I left home: *Show Pharaoh what the women of Babylon are made of.*

I had repeated her words to myself so many times when I first came to Egypt. They gave me strength as I adjusted to a new country and a new people. As I tried to make a life for myself here. What kind of life would it be now, with what I knew?

I reached deep inside myself, seeking calmness and strength. *Be what he expects you to be,* Ahmose had said. *Nothing more and nothing less.* I wasn't even quite sure I understood what she meant.

We stopped at the end of the hallway leading to the chamber where Pharaoh dined when he visited the Palace. Ettu and Sehener straightened my gown and wig before we continued. As we walked past the row of guards whose faces were now somewhat familiar to me, I caught the eye of one. He had taken me back to my palanquin the night I went to Pharaoh's palace and spoke to me kindly. I had been too distressed to thank him that night, and too surprised when I recognised him the next time. I stopped in front of him.

"I wanted to thank you," I said.

If he was surprised, he didn't show it, but then Pharaoh's personal guards were probably so well trained that nothing surprised them. He gave me a small nod, but made no further reply. I moved on, not wanting to cause trouble for him if he was seen with me. At the door, a guard ran his hands over my body to check for weapons, although what manner of implement I might hide beneath my gown was still a mystery to me. Then I was permitted to enter the chamber.

I had never dined alone with Pharaoh and I hadn't expected tonight to be any different, but to my surprise, the only woman in the chamber was a servant. Her face was unfamiliar, but her attire was not. The women who served Pharaoh were always naked except for a woven girdle around the waist. The girdle this woman wore was dyed golden. I restrained my smile at the thought that I should complement her on her fine girdle.

"Wine, my lady?" she asked.

"Please."

With one last twitch of my gown, Ettu and Sehener went off to wait in the place where the maids usually stood. The serving woman brought me a goblet. She had filled it a little too high and her hands trembled as I took it from her, spilling a few drops onto my fingers.

"Oh, my lady, I am so sorry," she said. "Let me fetch a cloth."

She was gone before I could reply. When she returned, Ettu was there to take the cloth and wipe my hand, although I tried to wave her away.

"It is not seemly for you to do it yourself," she hissed at me. "What if Pharaoh were to come in while you were doing so?"

Pharaoh would be unlikely to even notice me until he was sitting down with a goblet, but I let her clean my hand. She had just finished when the door opened. Ettu hurried back to join Sehener in standing with her back to the wall.

However, it wasn't Pharaoh who had arrived. It was a slightly-built woman wearing a very fine gown of pale blue linen, almost the same colour as my own. Fortunately for her, her gown was a little looser and didn't impede her movements the way mine did.

She looked me up and down, and a crease appeared in her forehead as she noted the similarity in our gowns. Behind her followed a woman who looked much like her, although her gown was not as fine. A servant, I assumed.

"Hilde, is it not?" I asked.

"It is, my lady." Her voice was soft and her accent unfamiliar to me. Her gaze dropped to my gown again as she approached me.

"It would seem we may have used the same seamstress," I said.

I had intended it as a joke since she looked so worried, but she shook her head.

"Oh no," she said. "This was made for me before I came

here by an old Egyptian woman who lived nearby. She said it would be indistinguishable from one made in Egypt and it would seem she was correct. Should I go back to my chambers and change?"

"Of course not," I said. "Pharaoh probably won't even notice."

The serving woman came to offer Hilde wine, which she accepted with a polite smile. The woman handed her a goblet, managing not to spill it this time, and hurried back to her station.

The door opened again and I turned, thinking it might be another Ornament come to dine with Pharaoh. Instead, it was more serving women, clearly distinguished by their too-brief attire.

"I am Kassaya," I said to Hilde, realising she mightn't remember me from Panouk's fleeting introduction the night she arrived. "From Babylon. My father is Marduk-apla-iddina. He is the king."

Why did I feel the need to add that? Was I trying to point out that I was a princess? She probably was too.

"Well met, my lady." She dropped her gaze to the floor as she curtseyed. "I am Hilde from Britannia."

"You really don't need to do that," I said. "We are both Ornaments."

She nodded, but didn't reply. I was tempted to ask whether Belet-ili had been assigned to her, but didn't want to have to explain how she had served my sister. Not now, in these moments before Pharaoh arrived.

"I suppose this will be your first time meeting Pharaoh?" I asked instead.

Her gaze darted up to meet mine and her lips trembled as

she nodded again. I should warn her that Pharaoh was probably not the kind of man she anticipated. She probably expected him to be a wise and just ruler. An honourable man at the least. But I didn't know her, and I couldn't trust she wouldn't relay my comments to someone else. To the administrators, or even to Pharaoh himself.

"Your maid looks much like you," I said instead. Please Marduk, let them not be sisters. I couldn't bear it.

"My cousin," Hilde said. "Our fathers are brothers and we grew up together. We are like sisters, and when she heard I was to be sent to Egypt, she insisted on coming with me."

How could I not warn her now? But before I could say anything, the door opened and two guards entered. They prowled around the chamber, even though there was nowhere anyone could hide. One of them returned to the door and held it open.

"My lord," he said.

Pharaoh swept in. I watched Hilde's face, trying to gauge her reaction as she saw him for the first time. I was well accustomed to his appearance by now — the enormous belly which hung over the front of his *shendyt*, the way his jowls wobbled when he walked — but I hadn't forgotten my shock at realising he looked nothing like the other men around me. They were all well muscled and pleasing to the eye. Pharaoh's appearance was anything but attractive.

He planted his substantial behind on a couch and the serving women flocked around him, bringing wine and a footstool. I could feel Hilde's hesitation as she watched me, seemingly looking for a guide as to what she should do. I waited until the serving women returned to their station before I approached Pharaoh. Hilde was only a step or two behind me.

I prayed I wouldn't tear my skirt as I dropped to my knees, set my goblet on the floor, and lay on my belly. Hilde was quick to copy me. Pharaoh waited only a few moments before he bid us to rise. I snatched up my goblet and waited for him to speak.

"Well," Pharaoh said. He eyed Hilde as he took a swig of his wine. "And who might you be?"

Pain stabbed through my heart. They were the exact same words he said to Ishtar the first time he saw her.

From the corner of my eye, I saw Hilde curtsy.

"I am Hilde, my lord. Daughter of Marcas from Britannia. My father sent me here to prove his loyalty to you as you requested."

Although her words were entirely correct, beneath them I sensed a burning rage. Like me, Hilde had been sent to a foreign country by her king and father. Like me, she would have chosen a different path for herself if such a thing was possible. She, too, resented being possessed by this man who lazed in front of us and leered at her as he drained his goblet.

"Well," Pharaoh said again as his gaze travelled from Hilde's face down to the sandals peeking out beneath her hem.

Should I say something? It might draw his attention away from Hilde. I could feel how she withered beneath his stare. How she wished she was anywhere but here. Or maybe that was how I would feel if he looked at me like that. It didn't matter. No woman should be subjected to the leer of such a man. But before I could think of what to say, his gaze drifted over to me. He studied me as if trying to remember who I was.

"From Babylon," he said at last. "A daughter of Marduk-apla-iddina."

"That is correct," I said, belatedly adding "my lord".

He only looked at me.

"My name is Kassaya," I said. *My sister is Ishtar*, I wanted to say. *You must remember her. You murdered her.*

"Yes," he said, then turned his attention back to Hilde.

"Come sit beside me," he said, and his wave seemed to include me as well.

Hilde hesitated and I guessed she was trying to decide which side she should sit on. I already knew it was better to sit on his right as he held his goblet with that hand, leaving the other free to roam the thigh of whichever woman was unfortunate enough to sit on the other side.

I sat on his left. I didn't do enough to protect Ishtar. I would do what I could for Hilde. We settled ourselves on either side of Pharaoh. A serving woman had already come to refill his goblet and he took a long drink, seeming to drain half the wine at once. Then his hand was on my thigh, as I had expected. I held myself very still and tried to pretend I couldn't feel it.

He said nothing else and I assumed he waited for either Hilde or me to make conversation. I couldn't think of anything to say that didn't include Ishtar, so I said nothing.

"My father sends his best regards to you, my lord," Hilde said eventually.

Her voice was tentative and I guessed she must be wondering why he didn't speak to us. Why he didn't ask her anything about herself, or her journey here, or even when she had arrived. Why he just sat there and drank and edged his hand ever higher up my thigh.

"Very good," Pharaoh said.

We lapsed into silence again.

There were so many questions running through my mind,

but I could say none of them. *How did you kill her? Did she suffer, or was it fast? What happened to her body? Why did you do it? Why? Why? Why?*

I clamped my mouth shut, determined not to let the words escape me. I couldn't accuse him. Not yet. Not until Ahmose found a way to make him fear me.

CHAPTER 19

The three of us sat in silence. I held myself very still as Pharaoh's hand roamed my thigh, trying to pretend to myself that I didn't mind. One of his personal guards stood nearby, as always, while another was stationed beside the door. I accidentally caught the eye of the one by the door and he quickly looked away, fixing his gaze firmly ahead of him. It must be obvious to him I didn't want Pharaoh's hand on my thigh, but he would do nothing to help me. Not that I expected he would. There was no choice but to suffer it.

I wished it was Khaemmalu who stood there, rather than this man whose name I didn't know. He wouldn't be able to stop Pharaoh's wandering hand either, but his presence would be a comfort.

The man who had looked at me must be either the captain of Pharaoh's personal squad, or his second. One of the two men Khaemmalu said his friend didn't trust. I wished I knew which of the guards who lined the hallway outside the chamber was Khaemmalu's friend.

"Ah!" Pharaoh said. His hand finally left my thigh as he lumbered to his feet. "Dinner!"

Hilde and I followed him to the little tables. Serving women already waited with their platters. Pharaoh dropped onto a cushion with a grunt. The food was sumptuous as usual, and far too much for three people. I took a hen's leg, some baked root vegetables, and bread. Hilde copied me, taking exactly the same as I did. Perhaps the food here was strange to her. She might not even know what it was. I knew little of Britannia or its people, but I understood what it was like to be a stranger in a foreign land.

We ate in silence. Hilde set down her knife at one point and looked like she was about to speak. She caught my eye and I shook my head slightly. She returned her gaze to her plate and kept eating.

I wasn't sure what I had been trying to tell her. Not that she shouldn't speak, but perhaps that she shouldn't feel like she should make any effort at conversation. Perhaps I was urging her not to draw attention to herself. She didn't yet know it could be dangerous to catch Pharaoh's attention.

Pharaoh was still eating long after I had had enough. I toyed with my food, taking the occasional small bite and trying to pretend I was still eating. Hilde appeared to do the same. She is a smart woman, I told myself. She looks to those around her and copies them. Perhaps there was no need for me to warn her Pharaoh could be dangerous. No need to risk that she might tell an administrator, or even Pharaoh himself. The less attention I drew to myself, the better.

When Pharaoh finally got to his feet, I pushed my plate away and followed. A serving woman came to refill his wine yet again. She glanced at my goblet, but I had barely touched it since I arrived, so she didn't ask if I wanted more.

"What is that?" Pharaoh's voice boomed and I jumped.

He glared at me. At my throat. I raised my hand to touch my necklace and was startled to realise my fingers trembled.

"This?" I asked. "I have had it since I was a small girl."

"Why are you not wearing the necklace I sent you?" he demanded. "I'm told it was very fine."

"I— uh—" My mind was blank and I couldn't think of a single response. I hadn't expected him to notice what I wore.

"Take it off," he said. "It is cheap and ugly."

"It is my favourite," I said.

His gaze turned dark. I had said the wrong thing. He took a single step towards me and reached for my throat.

I flinched, expecting him to grab me — memories of Ishtar's bruised neck flashed through my mind — but he only took hold of the gem and tugged.

I stifled a cry as the cord bit into the back of my neck. The cord snapped and Pharaoh tossed my gem to the floor.

"You will not wear it again," he said with another glower. "You will wear the one I sent you."

My mouth wobbled and I knew I would burst into tears if I tried to speak, so I only nodded. I had been a fool to think he wouldn't notice. I had thought him too self-absorbed to pay any attention to what I wore, but of course he would look for such an expensive gift.

Pharaoh stormed back to the couch, draining his goblet as he went. I took a deep breath to steady myself, then followed him. What else could I do? I couldn't risk angering him further.

I didn't see where my gem landed when it fell. Was it broken? Not that it mattered. I would never see it again. I could hardly go scrabbling around on the floor to find it. That gem was one of my most treasured possessions. One of the few items I bought with me from Babylon. And now it was gone. I had worn it thinking it would give me confidence, never expecting Pharaoh to notice, but I had been a fool to bring such a precious item here tonight.

Pharaoh dropped onto the couch with a bellow of "wine!". Hilde and I looked at each other. I wasn't sure whether we were supposed to follow him and she looked like she was frozen in fear. I tried to give her a reassuring smile, but my mouth wobbled and for one horrifying moment, I thought I would burst into tears.

I took a deep breath and straightened my shoulders. *Show Pharaoh what the women of Babylon are made of*, Mother had told me, and that's exactly what I would do. I would never let him see how much he upset me. Not until he feared me.

With my head held high, I went to the couch. Hilde was at my side and she surprised me by dashing forward at the last moment to take the spot on Pharaoh's left. Surely she had realised why it was better to be on his other side. I hesitated, wondering whether I could signal her to move, but she met my eyes and the defiance in them surprised me.

She gave me a tiny nod, as if to say *we are on the same side and I will protect you as you protected me.* Then she smiled up at Pharaoh.

"My lord," she said. "Would you tell me about your palace? I have not yet had the pleasure of visiting, but I hear it is very fine."

She had chosen her subject well. Pharaoh launched into a lengthy description of golden window frames and electrum columns. I settled myself on his right and resolved to keep my mouth shut. I had angered him enough tonight. Anything more might well endanger both myself and Hilde.

It wasn't long before Pharaoh's hand began wandering

Hilde's thigh. If I leaned forward a little, I could see past Pharaoh's bulk to her face. I noted the tightness around her eyes as his hand edged ever higher. Her eyes widened and I guessed he had squeezed her leg, as he did to me. He seemed to know exactly where to dig his fingers into the flesh of a woman's thigh to cause the most pain.

Pharaoh's monologue about the fineness of his palace went on and on. I sipped my wine sparingly, but even so, I had finished it long before he stopped talking. A serving woman came to refill my goblet, but I waved her away. My bladder already felt uncomfortably full and we might be here for hours yet. I wasn't sure at what point it would be acceptable to leave, but I supposed it wouldn't be until Pharaoh indicated I could.

He solved the dilemma for me when he finally ran out of ways to describe his palace. He gave me a curt nod.

"You may go," he said.

I rose, eager to leave before he changed his mind. Hilde started to get to her feet, clearly assuming he meant both of us, but Pharaoh gestured for her to sit.

"Not you," he said to her.

She froze, halfway to standing. She met my eyes and the look in them seemed to beg me to help. What could I do, though? It wasn't like I could ask Pharaoh to let her leave with me. I tried to offer her reassurance with my eyes, but she looked away and sat down again. She raised her goblet to her lips and drained her wine before I had even stepped away.

Ettu and Sehener hurried after me. Hilde's cousin stayed at her post, her back against the wall. I pitied both Hilde for what she was about to endure, and her cousin for having to witness it.

The door closed behind us and I couldn't suppress the sigh

of relief that rushed out of me. I was free of him, although that was tempered by the knowledge that Hilde was still there. I prayed to Marduk she would be safe tonight. As long as her cousin wasn't sent away, she might be. Surely he wouldn't do whatever he had done to Ishtar that last night with a maid there to witness it.

I set off down the hallway, past the guards who still looked as alert as ever. My eyes met those of the one who had helped me and he gave me a look that seemed to be part relief and part horror. Then we were past the row of men. We reached the end of the hallway and hurried around the corner.

"Are you hurt?" Ettu asked once we were well away.

I guessed she meant had I been injured when Pharaoh tore the necklace from my throat. My heart hurt at the loss of my favourite gem, but it could have been worse. I raised my hand to touch the back of my neck, where the cord had cut into my skin before it broke. It was tender, but there was no wetness, so it wasn't bleeding.

"I'm fine," I said. "I am worried for Hilde, though."

Ettu sighed. "I know, but there is nothing you can do for her."

"I should have warned her."

There had been time before Pharaoh arrived. Not enough time to tell her everything I knew, but I could have warned her that some women disappeared after spending time with Pharaoh. It would have been enough.

"Warned her?" Sehener repeated. "Whatever do you mean, my lady?"

When I hesitated, she hurried on. "Oh, I don't mean to be presumptuous. You obviously don't need to explain yourself to me."

I sighed, my heart heavy at the knowledge that I did need

to explain. We were not in the habit of watching what we said within the privacy of my chambers and I didn't want to start. I had invited Sehener to join us because I thought we could trust her. That meant she needed to know what we knew.

"Not here," I said. "This is best discussed where we can be assured of privacy."

"Of course," she murmured. "I do apologise. I was far too forward."

"Don't apologise," I said. "We all speak our minds within the privacy of my chambers. Don't we, Ettu?"

Ettu only huffed and when I glanced at Sehener, she seemed to be restraining a smile. We passed a servant woman who had obviously not seen Ettu's new manner of dressing, and who was so shocked, she actually stopped walking and stood in the middle of the hallway, staring. It was only when we were right in front of her that she gathered herself.

"I apologise, my lady," she murmured to me as she stepped aside.

"Do you feel like you had a good enough look?" Ettu asked coldly.

The servant woman's eyes were round and she looked from Ettu to me, seemingly lost for words. I walked on, and Ettu and Sehener followed me.

"If the stares bother you, why do you still dress like that?" Sehener asked once we were out of the woman's hearing.

"Why shouldn't I?" Ettu countered. "Is there some law that says only a man may wear a *shendyt*?"

"Well, no," Sehener stammered, and it took her a few moments to gather her thoughts. "I have been wondering why you wear it, though. We all have."

I wasn't sure whether she meant all my lady's maids or everyone in the palace. Perhaps it was both.

"And given how much everyone stares and how they talk about it, why you still do it," she added.

"I started because of the thing you found out about," Ettu said, making her reference to Tall discreet. "And because of that, it has been useful for me to continue dressing like this. But also, I find I like it. It is very freeing. I feel like a different person when I dress like a man."

"But does it not bother you, the way folk stare and gossip?" Sehener pressed.

Ettu took a little while to answer and I guessed she must be searching for the most truthful response.

"It does," she said at last. "But only a little, and I find I care less as time goes by. I have realised the world will not change unless we force it to, and I, for one, have decided I shall dress to please myself and nobody else. If folk I barely know choose to stare or they think me odd, it shall not bother me. Those who are closest to me, who share my lady's chambers, don't think anything of it, so why should I care what anyone else thinks?"

"You are very brave," Sehener said as we turned down the hallway to my chambers. "I hardly fathom how you can take such a view, but I do admire it."

"There are far more important things to concern ourselves with than what a woman chooses to wear," Ettu said. We stopped at my door and she knocked on it. "As you will find out."

CHAPTER 20

$\mathcal{I}$ studied Sehener's face as we waited for someone to open the door to my chambers. She was like Merytre in that both were accomplished at not letting their emotions show, unlike Ettu whose face and body always told me when she was unhappy, even if she didn't voice it. I suddenly realised I knew nothing about Sehener other than what I had observed while she was attending to me.

"Sehener, how long have you worked here?" I asked.

"Almost three years," she said. "Since I was eleven."

So she was fourteen. A year younger than me and two years younger than Ishtar. Or, rather, two years younger than Ishtar would be, if she still lived. My heart ached.

Merytre finally opened the door. Presumably the delay was because she needed to lock Tall away first. Her gaze went straight to my throat, where my pendant should have been. Ettu murmured something to her and Merytre only nodded, swiftly closing the door behind us before hurrying off to let Tall out. He followed her back out to the sitting chamber, and he and Sehener seemed to eye each other warily.

"I suppose you have to hide away every time the door is opened?" she said to him.

Tall glanced from Sehener to me, although I couldn't guess what he was thinking. Maybe he wondered how to respond to her, or maybe he wondered why she even spoke to him in the first place. Folk were not usually so quick to talk to Tall once they noticed his differentness. His mouth worked as he tried to find a response.

"Hide!" he said at last, managing again to use the Egyptian language. He bobbed his head at her, almost a little bow, then went to sit down.

Sehener followed and sat beside him. She smoothed her gown over her knees and gave him a companionable smile.

"It must be fearsome for you," she said. "Always having to worry that someone will find you."

Tall studied her.

"You!" he said.

"Yes, I did," she said. "But I am no threat to you. I am loyal to my lady and if she calls you a friend, that is good enough for me."

Tall didn't respond and the silence stretched between them as they stared into each other's eyes. Eventually Ettu cleared her throat.

"My lady, I retrieved this for you," she said and held out my yellow gem.

"Oh." I took it from her, surprised to notice my fingers trembled. There was a new chip in the wooden setting, but the gem itself seemed undamaged. "How did you find it?"

"It landed under one of the tables," she said. "I fetched it when you went back to the couch."

"Thank you." I sat down and set the gem on the arm of the couch. "I thought I would never see it again."

"What happened?" Merytre asked. "Did the cord break?"

"Pharaoh tore it from her neck," Ettu said, sitting down with a sigh. "He was incensed she didn't wear the gem he sent her."

"Are you hurt?" Merytre asked me. "Should I wake Ahmose? She went to bed shortly after you left, but you know she will not mind."

"No, let her sleep," I said. "My neck is a little sore, but it is probably only bruised. I will have her look at it in the morning."

"My lady." Sehener had finally managed to drag her gaze away from Tall. "You said you would tell me what you wanted to warn Lady Hilde about."

"Lady Hilde was there?" Merytre asked. "To dine with Pharaoh?"

"Yes, and she was still there when I left." My tone was grim. "I wouldn't have left her alone with him, but he sent me away."

"He probably wants to bed her," Sehener said. "She is young enough that she has probably never been bedded…"

Her voice trailed away as she studied us.

"What is it?" she asked. "There is something I don't know, isn't there? You look… afraid."

"As should you be," Ettu said in the brisk voice she always used for unpleasant news. "If you have been here for three years, you cannot be unaware of the rumours."

"Rumours?" Sehener repeated. "You mean the women who disappear, I assume? Of course I have heard the stories, but the administrators say—"

"The administrators lie," Ettu said.

"Or at least Amankhau does," Merytre added. "We aren't sure about Panouk yet."

"I don't think Panouk is involved," I said. "But I am absolutely certain Amankhau is."

"Involved?" Sehener's face showed her confusion as she glanced around at us. "Involved in what?"

"Danger!" Tall said. "Pharaoh!"

Sehener shook her head. "No, you must be mistaken. Pharaoh doesn't have anything to do with the women who left. They returned to their families."

How had Sehener understood Tall so immediately? Even I, who had always prided myself on how well I understood his often obscure statements, hadn't made sense of what he was trying to tell me until it was too late.

"I'm afraid there is much more to the story than you have been told," I said. "We have evidence that sometimes the women who meet privately with Pharaoh are—"

My voice broke and I could only shake my head. I couldn't say it.

"What my lady means to say," Ettu said quickly. "Is that the women who spend time with Pharaoh do not always survive the encounter."

Sehener's eyes were round.

"No," she said. "That cannot be true."

"Pharaoh!" Tall's voice was sad now.

"How do you know?" Sehener directed her question to Tall and even through my sorrow, it pleased me to see her treat him as if he could actually answer her question.

Tall touched his hand to his ear.

"You heard something?" she asked. "You overheard someone talking about it?"

He nodded and raised his hands to flap them. It was something that always made folk back away from Tall, as if they might catch whatever made him flap like that. But

Sehener only watched and waited patiently for him to speak.

"Pharaoh!" he said. "Guard!"

"Oh, my." Sehener turned back to me. "Is this... your sister... Lady Ishtar?"

"Yes." I had managed to compose myself somewhat while she was preoccupied with Tall, and my voice was calmer now. "We believe Pharaoh is responsible for my sister's disappearance. We were able to trace her movements that night as far as the chamber where she dined with Pharaoh."

Between us, we shared with Sehener what we had pieced together about Ishtar's disappearance. How she had been summoned to Pharaoh's palace to dine with him. How we confirmed she did indeed reach Pharaoh that night, and that most of his guards were sent off duty before she left. That Khaemmalu's friend believed Pharaoh mistreated some of his women, and that his captain and second disposed of the bodies for him.

"And now Half has returned to Pharaoh's palace to try to learn more," Ettu said when we had told Sehener everything else.

"The danger to him must be great," Sehener said, before directing her next words to me. "He must be very loyal to you, my lady, as are all your closest companions. I hope you will count me amongst them."

I nodded, but as always when someone professed their loyalty to me, I couldn't find the right words to reply. I had never expected to be the one folk offered loyalty to. I was only my father's youngest daughter. I was nobody important. It took me too long to figure out how to reply to Sehener, and by then she probably didn't expect a response anyway, but I felt I still needed to give her one.

"Thank you," I said to her. "I hope you will prove my trust in you is not unfounded."

It was a weak reply, and unworthy of her fine comment, but it was all I could think of in that moment. Ishtar, no doubt, would have made a more appropriate reply.

CHAPTER 21

Although I rose shortly after dawn the following day, Merytre was already up and Sehener had arrived. I supposed she would move in once Merytre went to Sutem's house. Sehener bustled about, seemingly tidying, although I couldn't see that what she did made much difference. Tall was in his usual spot to the side of the window. I was surprised to see him up so early.

Merytre sat on the couch, her needlework in her lap. She and Sehener were chatting quietly as I entered, although Sehener didn't stop her tidying.

"Sehener, you do not need to do that," I said. "There are servants who come twice a week to clean."

"I don't know what else to do with myself," she said. "I have only been here to dress you before. There must be other tasks you expect of your lady's maids?"

"Not really," I said, going to stand beside Tall at the window. "Ettu and Merytre occupy themselves with stitching, but that is their choice. I need someone to accompany me when I go out, but other than that…"

My voice trailed away as I wondered whether there was something else I was supposed to ask of my maids.

"What else would you expect to do?" I asked her.

"Well." Sehener paused to think. "I suppose I might polish your gems. And check your gowns for any repairs that are needed. Clean your sandals."

"And once you have done that?" Because surely those were tasks that only needed to be done occasionally.

"I could dust, or polish the floor, or stitch a new gown for you."

"But there are servants to do all those things."

A guard made his way around the perimeter of the grounds, although from this distance I couldn't see who it was. It could be Sutem. He would be on duty by now. Since I could see nothing interesting outside, I sat on the couch. Sehener hadn't replied, so I figured she was still trying to come up with other tasks she could do for me.

"Sit down, Sehener," I said. "You may as well relax."

Tall also left the window and perched on his favourite couch. Sehener followed, settling herself beside him and not seeming at all bothered by his nearness. He flapped his hands — perhaps Sehener made him nervous — but when she took no notice, he seemed to calm down. Soon he even stopped his flapping.

"I am quite good at stitching," Sehener said to me. "If you want something sewn, I am happy to do it for you."

"You were assigned to the sewers, weren't you?" Merytre asked. "My lady, there probably needs to be a message sent to let them know Sehener won't be working there anymore. Assuming, that is—"

I raised my hand for her to stop. "Of course she won't be working with them. Would you go later today to tell Panouk or whoever the most appropriate person is? You can advise him I have requested Sehener attend to me all day from now on."

Merytre gave a little nod.

"And I will speak with Sutem today," I added, not wanting her to think I had forgotten.

She coloured and looked down at her hands. I noticed she was wearing the finger ring she had chosen.

"Thank you, my lady," she said. "I showed him my finger ring, but I didn't tell him about the other one." She darted a glance at me. "In case you wanted to change your mind."

"Why would I change my mind?" I had already offered the finger ring. I couldn't understand why she might think I would take it back.

Merytre shrugged and stammered.

"I think," Sehener said, "what Merytre means to say is that you are so different to the other Ornaments, is all. They think nothing of making a promise and then breaking it. We are only servants, after all. There is no consequence for a promise broken to a servant and nobody would even think badly of a lady for it."

"I would," I said.

"But why?" Merytre asked. "What happened to make you so different? Is this what all Babylonian women are like?"

I pondered her question, searching for an answer. I had always been different, but never in a way anyone thought was good. The only friends I'd ever had were those who were considered odd by everyone else, like Tall and Half.

"I think it is just me," I said at last. "Maybe I don't understand how things should be done."

"There is absolutely nothing wrong with being a person who keeps their word," Ettu said from the doorway. She yawned even as she gave me a pointed look. We had probably woken her with our chatter. "You should be proud of having such a firm sense of right and wrong."

"Like when you refused to spread your own gossip," Merytre said. "When you found out folk were…"

Her voice trailed away, as if she suddenly questioned the wisdom of reminding me of that matter.

"When you found out folk were talking about you," Ettu finished for her.

"I have heard nothing of it," Merytre said. "If anyone is talking about you, they have not done so within my hearing."

As if anyone would speculate about whether I had something to do with my sister's disappearance while one of my own maids listened.

"Actually," Sehener said hesitantly. "There has been some talk. Tuya mentioned it to me. She overheard two of the kitchen servants. She told them in no uncertain terms that you had nothing to do with the matter."

"And that is exactly what any of us would do if we heard something," Ettu said.

When my maids came to dress me that morning, they seemed unusually chatty. At first, I paid no attention, but then Sehener made a comment to one of the women, who turned her back and didn't respond. Sehener's face was carefully blank, hiding her feelings, but I noticed she didn't try again to speak to any of them, and they seemed to pointedly ignore her.

"They are upset with Sehener," I said to Ettu once the other maids had left.

She and I had returned to the sitting chamber, while Merytre went to unlock Tall's door. Sehener was still in my bedchamber, packing away the cosmetics.

"They are jealous," Ettu said. "They obviously noticed she was already here when they arrived and have probably guessed you offered her a bedchamber. It will all settle in a few days. Best to let Sehener handle it herself if she thinks anything should be said."

I nodded, although I wanted to disagree. I didn't like my maids ostracising Sehener over such a thing. I understood why they would be jealous, but surely it wasn't worth being cruel to her about it. I would take Ettu's advice, though, and leave the women to sort it amongst themselves. In the meantime, I had something I needed to do anyway.

"I will go speak with Sutem now," I said.

I hesitated, wondering whether I should ask Merytre to come with me. The look on her face suggested she was trying to anticipate whether I expected her to come.

"Sehener and I will accompany you," Ettu said decidedly.

Merytre didn't object, so I assumed she was happy enough to not be there for such a conversation. She barred the door behind us as we left. As we reached the bottom of the stairs, I spotted Hilde. She approached from another direction, but looked as if she too was on her way out. A maid trailed behind her.

"Hilde," I called before I could think better of it.

She startled, and when she saw it was me who had called her, she ducked her head and hurried out the front doors.

"That was strange," Ettu said.

"I thought the two of you seemed quite friendly at dinner," Sehener added.

"So did I."

After all, she had deliberately positioned herself on Pharaoh's left after he tore the pendant from my neck, and I had thought she did it to protect me the way I protected her earlier. Maybe something had happened after I left. I didn't let myself wonder what manner of something it might be.

"She is not that far ahead of us," Ettu said. "You could still catch up to her."

"Come on then," I said.

We hurried after Hilde and I made sure not to forget to greet Khaemope and Karpusa at the front doors. Hilde was already quite a way ahead of us. She strode quickly as if she had a particular destination in mind. Her maid — the cousin who had attended her the previous evening — was almost jogging to keep up.

"Hilde," I called after her. "Please wait."

If she heard me, she gave no sign of it, only continued her fast pace.

"Please," I called again.

Hilde finally stopped, although she didn't turn around. I hurried to her, half-expecting she would change her mind and keep going.

"Hilde," I said, a little breathless by the time I reached her. "Why didn't you stop when I called to you?"

"I stopped," she pointed out curtly, although she still didn't turn to face me. "Otherwise we would not be here to have this discussion."

"Are you angry with me?" I asked, confused by her unfriendliness. Last night, we had seemed to be allies.

Hilde let out a huff and finally turned to face me. My gaze was immediately drawn to the marks at her throat. I stared at them for a long moment before I let myself meet her eyes. She glared at me and I was relieved to see her spirit was unbroken, despite whatever she had endured at Pharaoh's hands.

"You knew," she said bitterly. "You left me alone with that monster."

"He told me to leave." I knew how weak I sounded even as the words came out of my mouth.

"You should have warned me," she said. "I could have left before he—"

She stopped abruptly and covered her mouth with her hand. I thought she would burst into tears, but Hilde was obviously made of stronger stuff. Her cousin moved closer and set a hand on Hilde's arm, glaring at me all the while. Hilde took a moment to compose herself, then gave me a venomous look.

"I froze," she said. "When he put his hands to my throat, I couldn't even move. Had you told me, I could have been prepared. I would have fought back."

My mouth opened and closed. How did one respond to such a statement?

"I have already written to my father," she continued. "I have asked him to send for me. I will not stay here."

"You sent a message through Pentau?" I asked. "The Palace scribe?"

"Of course." She gave me another fierce glare. "Since it appears I am not permitted to write to my father myself."

"Pentau won't send such a letter," I said. "I'm sorry."

"Of course he will," she said. "He came to my chambers and wrote down my words. The message will be sent to my father and he will summon me immediately. He will send an escort to take me home. I only have to suffer this place until they arrive."

"What you told the scribe is one thing," I said. "What he writes may well be another. Any letter you send through Pentau will say only how grateful you are to have been sent here."

"That is not what I told him to write."

But she seemed a little uncertain now, as if she felt there might be some truth to what I said, but didn't want to believe it.

"Your letters to your father will never be anything but a glowing account of your life here," I said.

It was Tiye's maid, the one who locked me in when I refused to clean her bathing chamber, who told me that. Until then I, too, had thought I could inform my father of what things were really like here, although at that point I hadn't known what secrets the Palace hid. Even now, I wasn't sure I fully comprehended them. As awful as what I knew was, could there be even more I didn't yet know?

Hilde gave an exasperated huff.

"I will not tolerate that," she said. "I will summon the administrator and demand to write my own letter."

"He won't send it," I said. "If he says he will, it will only be to appease you."

"Then how am I supposed to communicate with my father?" Hilde stomped her foot and glared at me as if it was my fault. "Or must I walk right out the front gates and secure my own transport home?"

"I suppose you could try."

She would need Panouk's approval, but he had said he would send me home if I asked. I assumed he would do the same for any Ornament. I could hardly tell Hilde there was a more secret way out, using Ahmose's special potion.

"Does he do this to everyone?" Hilde asked.

I took a deep breath and tried to find the right words. As terrible as what she already knew was, there was so much more she didn't know.

"Oh, there is Sutem," Ettu said suddenly, tugging at my

arm. "My lady, don't forget you have most pressing business to discuss with him this morning."

"I will find him shortly," I said, shaking off her hand. Surely she understood this conversation with Hilde was more important than what I came to say to Sutem.

"But you were most insistent it couldn't wait another hour," Ettu said.

I shot her a sharp look. I had never said such a thing, so if Ettu claimed I had, there was a reason for it. But I had to tell Hilde what she should know. I would never forgive myself if I didn't and she suffered the same fate as Ishtar.

"Perhaps you and Sehener could go see him," I said. "Tell him to wait for me."

"But what if he asks what you intend to discuss?" Ettu widened her eyes at me, clearly trying to signal something important. She shot Sehener a look as if asking for her help.

"You know what I want to talk about," I said. "And I'm sure he does, too."

"He is almost out of sight, my lady," Sehener said. "You will need to hurry if you wish to speak with him today."

With one of them on each side of me, they urged me away from Hilde.

"Stop." I pulled my arms from their grasp. "Go tell Sutem to wait for me. I wish to speak with Hilde privately."

"But—" Ettu started.

I glared at her and she ducked her head in acknowledgement. She and Sehener hurried away in pursuit of Sutem without another word.

"What in the name of the goddess was that about?" Hilde asked. Her glare hadn't lessened.

"They think it would be unwise for me to answer your question," I said.

"Will you then?"

"Yes." I paused, searching for the right words before realising there was no gentle way to tell her. "No, he doesn't do that to everyone. He has never done it to me. But he did to my sister."

Her glare softened a little.

"I heard your sister left not long ago," she said.

"She didn't leave," I said.

Hilde met my gaze evenly.

"I heard you had her sold into slavery," she said. "That she was sent to the gold mines at your request."

"Lies," I said. "As is anything else you have heard about me being responsible for her disappearance."

Hilde studied me for a few moments.

"I believe you," she said. "I don't think you are telling the whole truth, but I do believe her disappearance was not at your instigation."

"She was murdered." I looked her in the eyes, willing her to understand what I hadn't said.

"My condolences." Hilde's anger seemed to dissipate and she pressed her hand against my arm.

Even now, I couldn't make myself say it. She already knew there was danger from Pharaoh, but there was no way she could have realised just how grave the danger was. She thought he would only hurt her. She didn't expect he might kill her. Even if I told her, there was nothing she could do with that information. Pharaoh would still do whatever he wanted. Perhaps I shouldn't give her that kind of fear. Let her live her life here and make of it what she could.

"Will you tell me what happened?" I asked, letting my gaze fall to her throat where four red lines marked where he had grabbed her. Just like the marks I saw on Ishtar's neck the first time Pharaoh abused her. Why did he do that to Ishtar and to Hilde, but not to me?

Hilde looked away. Her throat worked as if she swallowed hard. At length, she shook her head.

"If you cannot see fit to tell me what I should have known, then I have nothing further to say to you," she said.

Then she turned away and strode off. Her cousin hurried after her, but not before shooting me a look that was equally fierce as Hilde's.

CHAPTER 22

There seemed no point in chasing after Hilde. She had made it clear she didn't want to speak with me. I should have found a way to warn her earlier and it shamed me I hadn't tried hard enough. Ettu and Sehener had caught up to Sutem by now, and the three of them watched me. Straightening my shoulders, I went to them, although speaking with Sutem was the last thing I felt like doing right now. Had I been alone, I probably would have cried. But I wouldn't let my disappointment in myself interfere with my promise to Merytre.

"My lady." Sutem bowed, but not before I saw the wary expression on his face.

I gave him a stern look. Although I was on friendly terms with him, I was here to negotiate a marriage contract since Merytre had no father to do it for her. I didn't think any father would start such a discussion with amiability.

"Sutem," I said. "Merytre tells me you wish to marry her."

If he was at all fazed by my launching straight into the conversation, he hid it well.

"I do, my lady," he said. "She is the most remarkable woman I have ever met. I knew from my first conversation with her that we would be a good match. It took me a while to persuade her, though."

He gave a little chuckle which, under other circumstances, I might have found endearing. I didn't let myself smile, though, and only continued to stare at him. He didn't fidget or display any other sign of awkwardness. His composure impressed me. He was a calm, steady man.

"Do you love her?" I asked.

He met my eyes. "I do, my lady."

"And you have a sufficient income to provide for her?" I asked. "I would not see her marry into poverty."

"Yes, my lady. Pharaoh places the highest importance on the safety of his Ornaments and we are paid very well for our services. Merytre and I won't be living in luxury, but she will never want for anything she needs."

What else should I ask? What would a father ask?

"You can protect her?" I asked. "Keep her safe?"

It was a daft question and I realised immediately. Of course he could. He was a guard at the Palace of the Ornaments. He had probably received the very best training.

"Of course, my lady," he said quickly. "Those of us who patrol the grounds here are well trained, and I served at Pharaoh's palace for two years before I transferred here. I even worked in his personal squad for a time."

"Why did you leave that position?"

Did Sutem know about Pharaoh's culpability for the missing women? Surely he at least suspected. But if he did, he gave no sign of it, and when he spoke, his voice was as easy as ever.

"It didn't suit me, my lady," he said. "The hours are very

long and there is often little time to sleep between shifts. It was no life to offer a wife, and although I hadn't yet met a woman I wanted to marry, I hoped it would be something that might be in my future."

I supposed I couldn't expect him to volunteer anything he knew. He didn't know whether he could trust me.

"Merytre would not need to work," Sutem said. "My income is enough for us to live on, but she says she will not leave her position with you, and I accept that. I will wait at the gates for her at the end of my shift each day, so she won't be walking home alone after dark."

I nodded, still trying to figure out what else I should ask.

"And, of course, I do not expect a bride price for her," he added. "I know she has no family to provide such a thing. I only wish to be able to marry her and I care nothing for anything else."

I glanced at Ettu, thinking she might prompt me if there was something else I should ask, but she shrugged. Of course, she had never married herself, so she probably knew no more than I did. The look on Sehener's face said she was no more likely than Ettu to offer anything I had forgotten.

"Very well then," I said, fishing in my pouch. "I give my permission for her to marry you."

"Thank you, my lady." Sutem's relief was palpable. "I honestly wasn't sure you would approve of me."

"Why not?" Had I missed something that indicated he was not a suitable match for Merytre?

"I didn't know whether you would consider a mere guard to be of high enough status for a lady's maid. I will look after her well, my lady."

I retrieved the finger ring Ettu had selected from my pouch, and held it out to him. Sutem's eyes widened.

"My lady?" For the first time in our conversation, he sounded uncertain.

"Merytre's bride price," I said. "I trust this will be sufficient?"

Sutem seemed to swallow hard.

"My lady, I can't accept that," he said. "It is far too valuable. I knew there would be no payment. I am not marrying her in the hope of riches. I just want to be with her."

"Take it, Sutem," I said. "I told Merytre I would negotiate her marriage contract and my understanding is that the customs of her people require a bride price."

He took the finger ring from me and I would have sworn his hand trembled a little. He studied it, turning it until the red gem caught the sun.

"My lady," he said. "This is… I don't even know what to say."

"You may do as you wish with it," I said. "Although my advice would be to keep it somewhere safe in case you ever have need of such an asset."

"I will," he said. "If something should happen to me, this would provide for Merytre for the rest of her life."

It pleased me that his first thought was of her, and not of a life of luxury for himself.

Unsure of how to end the conversation, I gave him a nod.

"Treat her well, Sutem," I said. "I will have much to say to you if you don't."

I left him standing there, gaping at the finger ring.

"That was very well done," Ettu said as we headed back to the Palace.

"Why did you try to stop me from telling Hilde?" My tone was somewhat shorter than I had intended.

A sideways glance at Ettu as I spoke showed her shoulders had stiffened.

"We don't know whether she can be trusted," she said.

"She has no loyalties here yet," I said. "No reason to tell anyone."

"That doesn't mean she won't," she said. "And she already blames you for not warning her. That is not rational, and it makes me wonder what she might do if provoked."

"I agree with Ettu," Sehener said. "Lady Hilde is new and she will want to develop alliances. The information you have given her could be useful in that."

"I have done no more than I wish someone had done for me when I arrived," I said.

If someone had warned me, I would have sent Ishtar away as soon as Pharaoh showed his interest in her, or I would at least have tried to. If Panouk didn't allow her to leave, she could have taken Ahmose's potion and slipped away secretly. She would still be alive, even if it meant she had to make a new life for herself somewhere else. I probably never would have seen her again, but at least she would have lived. There hardly seemed any point in thinking such a thing, but I couldn't help it. I could have saved her.

"We should be helping each other, not trying to compete," I said.

"It's not about competition," Ettu said. "I fear you told her to make yourself feel better, but what if Lady Hilde were to tell the administrators? Is the warning to her really worth the risk?"

"What if she tells Pharaoh?" Sehener added.

"She won't," I said, trying to sound more confident than I felt.

"How can you be sure?" Ettu asked.

I remembered the look on Hilde's face as she took my place on Pharaoh's left. She might blame me for not warning her about Pharaoh's cruelty, but she could never say I hadn't tried to protect her. And now she had experienced his brutality, she had no reason to trust him.

"I just know it," I said.

CHAPTER 23

Several days after I gave Ahmose Ishtar's gem, she sidled up to me in the sitting chamber as I poured myself a drink. The others lazed on the couches, seemingly more asleep than awake.

"I must speak with you," Ahmose murmured. "In private."

I gave her no more than the slightest nod, not wanting to rouse anyone's suspicion, and took my drink back to the couch. It wasn't until late afternoon, when the day finally started to cool, that I announced I would take a walk.

"Ahmose, would you accompany me?" I asked.

She got to her feet with a groan. I would have felt bad about asking her if I didn't know she was waiting to talk with me.

"I can go with you," Ettu said quickly. "Let Ahmose rest."

"No, no," Ahmose said. "I am quite fine."

She hobbled to the door and Ettu came to bar it behind us. We made our way through the Palace and I walked much slower than usual, mindful of Ahmose's age. She seemed to be breathing more heavily than was warranted for such a slow pace.

"Are you well?" I asked her.

"Yes." Still, she sounded breathless, even with so brief a reply.

"We don't have to go outside. We could talk here."

"I will manage."

Still, I walked even slower, not liking the way she was breathing. We eventually made it outside and I headed for a private spot where I remembered seeing a wooden bench. Ahmose said nothing until we were seated.

"My contact has spoken with Messui," she said.

"And?"

I couldn't read the look on her face. Had no idea whether she was about to tell me her contact had received a positive reaction from the librarian, or a negative one.

"As she thought, he is open to a bribe," she said.

"Has he been given the gem yet?"

"No. I showed it to my contact and she described it to Messui. But I said he must provide the information we seek before he receives it. He is amenable to that."

"How long will it take? And does he know which scroll has the spell I need?"

"He knows no more than that we seek spells of power. He will search the scrolls when he can, but he can only do it when Shotmaadje, the other librarian, isn't there. It may take some time, but I am confident of success."

I had hoped for more, but it would have to be enough for now. As much as I wanted the spell immediately, it would take time to find what I needed.

That night, I dreamed again of the lions and narcissus. I walked through the Palace grounds. My feet were bare and the grass beneath them was soft and damp. Somebody strode beside me, although I never saw who it was. We walked in silence.

As we passed a bed of narcissus, the flowers bowed down to me. I stopped walking.

"Why do you bow to me?" I asked the narcissus. "I am not a queen. I am not worthy of such obeisance."

"But you wish to be," said my unseen companion. "This place has corrupted you. You seek power and glory, but it will be your ruin."

Then a pair of lions stood on the other side of the flower bed. The narcissus unfolded from their bows and reached up to the sky, becoming an impenetrable field through which the lions could not pass.

I woke slowly and it took me some time to realise I no longer stood in the gardens, where the narcissus protected me from the lions. It was not the first time I had dreamed of the flowers protecting me. They spoke to me once in another dream, a message which I knew was important, but had never been able to recall.

Who was my unseen companion in this latest dream? Ahmose was the only person who knew of my desire to become powerful enough for Pharaoh to fear me, but the person who walked beside me didn't feel like her. Could it have been the seer with the scaled face? She had spoken to me once before in a dream. Told me to leave while I still could. Perhaps since I had ignored that message, she tried again to communicate with me?

But why would she? She didn't know me. We had met only the once and briefly. She had no reason to help me or warn me. How arrogant was I to think myself so important that a seer would send me secret messages in a dream? I rolled onto my side and closed my eyes, determined to return to sleep and forget my stupid thoughts about dream messages.

I slept restlessly after that and kept waking with the lingering memory of narcissus, although I wasn't sure whether I dreamed something new or if it was merely the memory of the flowers bowing down to me. As the bird outside my window began its dawn song, I was wide awake.

"I am going to sit with Tiye this morning," I said to Ettu, who was already in the sitting chamber when I entered. She sat on a couch and seemed to be doing nothing other than staring at her hands, which was unusual for her.

Ettu nodded, but didn't respond. When I looked at her more carefully, I noticed the paleness of her face and the tightness around her eyes.

"Ettu, are you unwell?" I asked.

She gave me a faint smile.

"No, my lady. Just worried."

"About Half?"

"Talking about him with you brought all my fears back. I am so afraid. If something has happened to him, we may not even hear of it. He could already be—"

Her voice choked and she stopped. I guessed she had been about to say Half could already be dead, and it wasn't an unreasonable fear. If Tall hadn't been with him when he was stabbed, Half wouldn't have survived. If Userhet saw him, he would undoubtedly go after him again. And this time he would be sure to do the job properly.

"Half will be careful," I said. "You know that. He is doing everything he can to ensure he returns safely to us."

"It may not matter how careful he is," Ettu said. "We have no idea how many people are involved in this thing, either there or here. It will only take one person to see him. One person who knows he knows a little more than he should, and they will go after him again. He will disappear and we will probably never know the truth of what happened to him."

Her voice choked again and she buried her face in her hands.

"That is exactly why I am going to see Tiye today," I said. "She knows more than she has said."

"You intend to confront her?" Ettu wiped away a few tears. "Do you think that is wise? You know some folk say she is involved."

"She has no more to do with it than I did with Ishtar's disappearance, but I am certain she knows something. I am going to find out what."

"I cannot say I think it is wise, but I also know I won't be able to talk you out of it."

"There is no danger to me from her," I said. "But if anyone can tell me what it is we don't yet know, it will be Tiye."

I decided to break my fast in my chambers, wanting to focus on what I intended to say to Tiye rather than making conversation with Hemetre. Since the marriage negotiations had now been concluded, Merytre had gone to Sutem's house last night, and Sehener slept in her old bedchamber.

Merytre arrived shortly after dawn, glowing in the way only a newly married young woman did, and greeted us cheerily. There was, Merytre had explained to me, no need for a marriage ceremony. A woman simply moved in with her new husband and they were then considered married.

The kitchen servants brought our morning meal. The others gathered around to serve themselves, but Sehener hesitated, eyeing the food with wariness.

"Is there nothing that takes your fancy?" I asked. "If you want something particular, just tell the kitchen I have asked for it and they will send it tomorrow."

"Oh." Sehener gave me a startled look. "That is most

generous of you, my lady. But I am only a servant. I am accustomed to eating whatever is provided."

"Then why do you hesitate?" I asked. "Are you not hungry?"

"Because…" She glanced at the food again. "I wondered what of it I am permitted to have."

I gave her a puzzled look.

"Whatever you wish," I said.

Ettu and Merytre were already eating. Tall took half a pomegranate and went to stand to the side of the window as he so often did. Ahmose hadn't yet emerged from her bedchamber, but there would be plenty of food left for her whenever she got up.

"Sehener, you will find my lady doesn't stand on ceremony within these chambers," Ettu said. She was comfortably ensconced on a couch with a bowl on her lap.

"But do you not wait until my lady has chosen what she wishes to eat first?" Sehener asked.

Ettu only shook her head, her mouth already full.

"If you want any gruel, you should have it while it's hot," Merytre advised Sehener. "It tastes like glue once it cools."

"And you know what glue tastes like how?" Ettu asked.

"Go ahead and eat," I said to Sehener. "I often can't eat in the morning these days, so you would be very hungry if you waited for me."

It was only after I said it that I realised I wasn't feeling ill for a change. Maybe the morning nausea had finally passed as Ahmose had said it would.

"But what if I eat whatever you wanted for yourself?" Sehener asked. "What if there is none left for you?"

I shrugged. "Then I will eat something else, or I will send someone to the kitchen to ask for more."

"But…" Sehener waved her hands towards the food.

"I understand," Merytre said. "It was all rather strange to me at first too, but my lady is different to the other Ornaments. You really won't be punished for eating, even if she hasn't."

Indeed, Ettu had already finished her gruel and went back to select some fruit. Sehener gave me one last cautious glance before she followed. I waited until she had taken what she wanted, before I served myself some bread and honey, not wanting her to think I really was trying to ensure she didn't take something I wanted.

While my maids bathed and dressed me a little later, I silently rehearsed what I would say to Tiye. It wouldn't be a conversation she welcomed, and she might well refuse to answer my questions, but I had to try. We needed to be sure we knew everything about the danger to us.

I didn't notice Abar until she pushed her way through my maids to stand in front of me. She held her head high and her eyes flashed a warning.

"Have you found my sister yet?" she demanded.

"Abar," Ettu said, a quiet rebuke in her voice.

"I have someone looking for her," I said. "Someone who has access to the lists that record where various women were sent."

"You've been saying you're looking for her for weeks," Abar said. "I don't believe you anymore."

"Abar, enough," Ettu said.

"Regardless of whether you believe me or not, I am doing what I can." I met her eyes evenly. "This is a very large place and things do not move swiftly. It has taken me some time to find someone who has the access we need in order to try to trace your sister."

"Try," she repeated scornfully. "You say you try, but I see no evidence of it."

"Abar, you may wait in the sitting chamber," Ettu said before I could reply.

Abar gave her a sullen look, but didn't move.

"Go," Ettu said.

Still Abar stood there. I held my tongue, knowing Ettu needed to manage the situation herself. She was in charge of my maids and if she saw fit to discipline one of them, I couldn't be seen to be interfering in that. With a huff, Abar turned and strode out. Ettu followed her.

"That's what happens when you bring in the ones who are upside down," one of the maids muttered. Khensa, perhaps. I still had trouble telling her from Hemetre, as both women had round faces and wore similar short wigs.

"What does that mean?" I asked, giving her a sharp look. I'd never heard such a thing before, but it sounded like an insult.

"Nothing, my lady." She fixed her gaze on the kohl bottle in her hand.

"Tell me," I said. "I want to understand."

"They are a backwards people," she said. "You know."

"I don't," I said. "Truly."

"They drink piss instead of beer," Tuya offered.

"And they eat faeces instead of food," added the other one with the round face and short wig. Hemetre, maybe.

"What nonsense," I said. "No people do such things, no matter where they are from."

The women only shrugged and avoided my eyes, even Merytre and Sehener. Baffled, I didn't pursue the conversation any further. Instead, I turned my focus to what I planned to say to Tiye, and my maids seemed relieved to let the matter drop.

As I made my way to Tiye's chambers a short time later, it felt like I couldn't quite catch my breath. I didn't know how she would react at being questioned. Right now, she was an ally to me, but she could be dangerous. I wasn't yet sure what it would take for her to feel she had been crossed.

Merytre and Sehener escorted me to the end of Tiye's hallway. Even though we were sure the danger lay in Pharaoh's palace, it seemed prudent to ensure none of us were alone. I couldn't forget the tales of women who were dragged from their chambers. If Amankhau was truly involved, then this place might be no safer than Pharaoh's palace.

A maid ushered me inside — Bennerib, I thought her name was — and a quick glance around showed no evidence of Nammu. That was a relief. I never liked to speak about anything meaningful if that woman was where she might hear us. Tiye sat on a cushion beside a little table littered with the remains of her morning meal. It looked much the same as what the kitchen servants had brought to my chambers. So, it seemed Tiye didn't receive anything special. I took an odd satisfaction in that knowledge.

"Good morning," she said to me. "You are rather early today."

"I'm sorry," I said. "I didn't realise it was so early."

I had been up since dawn after all.

"No matter." Tiye dipped her fingers in a bowl of water, wiped them on a linen cloth, then rose elegantly to her feet.

She moved to a pair of couches which faced each other and sat, gesturing for me to take the other. We looked at each other.

"Go on then," she said. "I can feel you are here to say something specific, so let's hear it."

Her forthrightness startled me and my carefully prepared speech fled.

"Have you met the new Ornament yet?" I asked instead.

"Hilde? Yes, she attends me early each morning." Tiye smirked at me.

Of course, Hilde would have been summoned to clean Tiye's bathing chamber every day. That duty had been Ishtar's most recently.

"I finally had a chance to speak with Pentau," Tiye said before I could ask anything further. "About your request."

"About Abar's sister? What did he say? Does he know where she is?"

"She was assigned to Pharaoh's palace. Laundry work. Apparently she speaks little Egyptian, so she was given a task where that wouldn't interfere with her ability to do her duties."

"So she is safe."

The relief that filled me was immense. I would be able to tell Abar that Atahar was working in Pharaoh's place. The two sisters might never have the opportunity to meet — after all, their respective positions gave them neither reason nor time to travel between the palaces — but I could at least tell her where her sister was.

"Thank you, Tiye," I said. "This will mean so much to Abar."

"You shouldn't make a habit of doing such favours for your servants. It sets them up to expect more than their station in life entitles them to."

I thought of Sehener's confusion about selecting food for herself if I hadn't yet eaten. No doubt Tiye always took the choicest items for herself, whether she wanted them or not. Or more likely, her maids ate in the servants' dining chambers.

We studied each other for a few moments. Now the time had come to confront her, I had forgotten what I planned to say.

"Something on your mind?" she asked.

I took a deep breath and readied myself.

"Do you remember what you told me when we talked about Nebtu?" I asked

She tipped her head to the side and studied me. Of course she wouldn't. We had probably discussed Nebtu several times. She wouldn't know which time I meant.

"You said if I knew something about Nebtu's disappearance, I should keep it to myself," I said. "That it would be dangerous for anyone to think I knew something."

Tiye nodded. "I remember."

"Is that why you didn't tell me what you knew? Because you thought it would be too dangerous?"

I held her gaze and she was the first to look away.

"And what is it you suppose I knew?" Tiye smoothed her gown over her knees, then draped one arm across the back of the couch, seemingly trying to pretend she was perfectly at ease with the conversation. The way she avoided my eyes told me she wasn't.

"I think you know exactly what happens to the women who disappear," I said. "All this time you've pretended you don't, but you do. You've known all along."

Tiye let her arm drop and sat up straight.

"Everybody out," she demanded with a wave towards the door. The two maids — Bennerib and another whose name I didn't know — scurried out. Tiye waited until the door closed behind them before she leaned forward and stared hard at me.

"Whatever it is you think you know," she said in a dangerous tone, "you should keep to yourself. This palace is full of secrets, and telling a secret that is not yours is never a wise move."

"Are you threatening me?" I met her stare and tried to pretend I felt bolder than I did. In truth, her voice and the way she looked at me made me quake. I had been so sure Tiye wasn't involved, but now it was only her and me in her chambers, and she was looking at me like a snake about to devour a rat, I wasn't so sure.

"I'm trying to protect you." Tiye leaned back and the feeling of danger dissipated. "Although you seem determined to put yourself at risk."

"I know what happens to them," I said. "And I think there are other folk who know as well. What I don't understand is why nobody does anything about it. If we all stood together—"

"Enough." Tiye got to her feet and strode over to the window. She stood looking out with her back to me. Maybe it was to give her a few moments to compose herself. When she turned around again, her face held no emotion. "Whatever grand secret you think you've uncovered is not the truth. The truth is almost too terrible to comprehend, and trust me when I say this, Kassaya, you do not want to know."

"It's Pharaoh," I said. "He kills them and his guards hide the bodies."

Tiye's eyes widened. I had shocked her. She had honestly believed I couldn't have uncovered the truth.

"What is the 'business' you didn't trust me to hear about?" I asked. "It has something to do with this, doesn't it? Do all the women who were at Ineni's gathering that night know?"

Tiye, Henutmire, Ineni, Gilukhipa, and Neferu. Five women who knew the truth, and none of them had told me.

"We could do something about it," I said. "We don't have to accept this."

Tiye came to sit down again. She stared at her hands in her lap for a long moment, before she raised her gaze to meet mine. She looked haunted and for the first time, I realised how the terrible secret she hid must weigh on her.

"I assume you think you could have saved your sister," she said. "You couldn't have. If Pharaoh summoned her, she had to go. There is no other option. What you know makes no difference to how you live your life here."

"I would have sent her away. If she wasn't here, she couldn't go to him."

"You still haven't figured it out, have you?" The look Tiye gave me now was strangely pitying. "We cannot leave this place. Any of us. Once you are sent here, you will remain here. Until Pharaoh tires of you."

"Panouk told me I could leave if I wanted to. That I only had to say it and he would arrange transport for me."

"Go try it," she said with a shrug. "Tell Panouk you want to return to your father and see what happens. He will argue with you, try to change your mind, make all sorts of promises about riches and extravagant gifts from Pharaoh. He will give you excuse after excuse. If you still insist you wish to leave, there will come a point where he will simply say you cannot. You may not. Once we enter the Palace of the Ornaments, we do not leave."

I knew we couldn't just stroll out of the gates whenever we

wanted, but I had honestly believed Panouk would send me home if I asked.

"You told me we would have villas in the city," I said, desperately now. "You said it yourself. That if we bore Pharaoh sons, we would retire and be given villas."

"It has happened," Tiye said. "I know of two Ornaments who retired with their own villas."

"Two?" My breath was strangely short now and my head swam. "Only two? Out of all the hundreds, thousands, of women who have lived here, only two have ever retired?"

"Two that I know of. That doesn't mean there weren't others."

"But what happened to everyone else?" I asked. "There must be more than two women here who…"

I couldn't make myself say the words. It was too horrifying. All the thousands of women who must have been Ornaments at one time or another, and Tiye was saying she knew of only two who left this place alive.

"There would be others," she said quickly. She eyed me warily, as if she expected me to do something unpredictable. "Some were probably permitted to return to their homes once their childbearing years were done. Others may have chosen to go somewhere else."

"But you don't know that," I said. "Not with certainty."

"No. All I can tell you is that if a woman lives long enough to get old, she… leaves."

"But you don't know they leave here alive."

She looked at me for a long moment, then gave a heavy sigh.

"No," she said at last. "But I cannot believe anything else. There are too many women."

Tiye herself must be near the end of her childbearing

years. Did she fear whatever fate approached if she was no longer useful to Pharaoh? Is that why she clung so fiercely to her position as Top Ornament and Pharaoh's Favourite? I sank back into my chair, overcome with the enormity of the situation. It was far worse than I had imagined. This was not only about Pharaoh's crimes against individual women. This might be about the fate of every single Ornament.

"I wasn't even supposed to be here." I was barely aware of the words that left my mouth.

"So why are you?" Tiye asked. "Why was the youngest daughter sent in place of the elder?"

"Ishtar got herself with child. She knew our father wouldn't send her if she carried another man's babe. Since the alliance was already made, Father had to send someone, and I was the only other option."

My anger at Ishtar was gone now, tempered perhaps by the knowledge that I would never see her again. In its place was only resignation and tiredness.

"And yet he sent her anyway," Tiye said. "But not until after he had sent you."

"She lost the babe."

Tiye nodded. She, of all people, understood how closely a woman's worth was tied with her ability to bear a child.

CHAPTER 25

"Where is Abar?" I asked as my maids crowded around me the following morning. They had already stripped me naked and forced me to endure their attentions in the bathing stall where they removed every last stubble of growing hair from my body. My skin was red from being scrubbed with natron until they were satisfied with my cleanliness. Now I was dressed and sitting on a stool in my bedchamber while they attended to my makeup and argued about which wig and jewels I should wear today.

The conversation with Tiye lay heavily on my mind. What we knew about Pharaoh's crimes was one thing. But now I knew every Ornament had something to fear, whether they came to Pharaoh's attention or not. But I hadn't forgotten what Tiye had learned about Abar's sister and I wanted to take the first opportunity to let her know.

"Abar," Ettu said. "My lady wishes to speak with you."

The girl pushed her way through the maids, who parted reluctantly with one muttered comment I didn't quite hear, but which seemed to be another slur against her heritage.

Abar stood in front of me, her face as sullen as always. She glared at me rather than looking respectfully at the floor as the servants here usually did, and made no apology for yesterday's outburst. I wondered, and not for the first time, what her circumstances had been before she was taken from her home. Her anger was unflinching and didn't seem to fade. There was no acceptance of her new situation. Not yet, at any rate.

"I have news of your sister," I said.

Abar's face changed, hope replacing the sullenness.

"Tell me," she said. "Where is she?"

"She was assigned to Pharaoh's palace," I said. "She works in the laundry."

The relief that crossed Abar's face made the indignity of having to ask Tiye for a favour — and the hairbrush it cost me — worthwhile.

"Good," Abar said. "I shall send her a message."

She turned and pushed through the maids again.

"Abar." Ettu's tone was short now and the girl didn't withhold her sigh. "You have not thanked my lady for what she did for you."

Abar didn't turn around, although she hesitated in the doorway. The maids' chatter died as we waited for Abar's response.

"She has done no more than she should," Abar said over her shoulder. "I should not have been parted from my sister in the first place. We should not have been taken from our homeland."

"My lady is not responsible for your situation," Ettu said. "And you will give her your sincere thanks immediately."

"I am a prisoner here," Abar shot back. "I do not owe anyone anything."

Ettu exhaled, a long, deep breath, perhaps intended to calm herself.

"We will discuss this in the sitting chamber," she said. "Excuse us, my lady."

She strode out and her footsteps retreated down the hallway. I thought Abar might actually refuse to go with her, but after a moment's hesitation, she followed with her head held high.

"Ungrateful wretch," one of the women said. Khensa or Hemetre.

"Hush," Sehener said. "Ettu will handle it and there is no need for any of us to comment."

She met my eyes and I gave her a small nod, hoping she would understand my gratitude, even if I wondered why she didn't say anything like that the last time the maids insulted Abar.

"Yes, well, you would say that, wouldn't you," Mutnofret muttered.

"What is that supposed to mean?" Sehener asked.

"I heard you have your own bedchamber," Mutnofret said. "Here in my lady's own chambers."

"Wonder what she did to earn that," Tuya muttered snidely.

"Enough," Merytre said. "You know Ettu would not tolerate such comments and they are no less acceptable because she cannot hear you. My lady bestows her favour as she chooses and it is not our place to question it or to speculate."

The women fell silent, apart from one cleared throat which sounded like a disagreement. I wondered why they felt free enough to say such things in front of me, but not Ettu. Perhaps they assumed I didn't listen to their conversations.

Or maybe it was because I didn't chastise them last time. That was only because I didn't understand their comments until they were explained to me. Perhaps I should have rebuked them afterwards.

When Ettu returned with Abar, who looked even more sullen than usual, she gave them a sharp look, obviously sensing something had happened in her absence. I saw Merytre catch her eye and shake her head just the tiniest bit, a warning not to ask perhaps. Ettu turned her attention back to Abar.

"Go on then," she said briskly.

"Ettu says I must thank you for finding my sister," Abar said.

She stared fixedly at the floor, and although her voice was anything but contrite, her words did at least sound somewhat respectful. Ettu gave Abar a pointed look. Apparently the girl had not said what she was supposed to.

"You are welcome," I said before Ettu could chastise her again.

"I must go." Abar was already on her way to the door.

"Abar—" Ettu started, but the girl was gone. She huffed, managing to convey both exasperation and displeasure in the one noise.

"Let her go," I said.

It was no more than I myself would do if I discovered Ishtar was somewhere nearby, safe and well. I would drop everything to contact her as soon as possible. I couldn't blame Abar for wanting to do the same.

In the dining chamber a little later that morning, I sat in my usual spot next to Henutmire.

"Kassaya," she said, eyeing me with a concerned expression. "Are you well?"

The serving women came to offer their platters and it was a little while before I was able to reply.

"Well enough," I said to Henutmire.

I had thought myself calm, but my chin wobbled as I spoke and I almost burst into tears. The secrets I carried suddenly felt like too much. The knowledge that Pharaoh himself was responsible for Ishtar's disappearance. The certainty that Amankhau was somehow involved. Tiye's claim there was no future in which we were permitted to leave the Palace after our childbearing years were done. How much of it did Henutmire know? How much did any of the other Ornaments know?

"No news then," Henutmire said.

I kept my gaze on my plate as I shook my head.

"I'm sorry," she added. "I cannot understand exactly how it must feel for you, but I do know something of the pain."

After all, Nebtu was her friend. I made a sudden decision to tell her what we had learned about the body of an unknown woman being taken to the House of Life. It could well have been Nebtu. She would want to know. I could tell her that much, at least.

"Henutmire," I said, leaning towards her.

"I have news of my own," she said, seemingly not realising I had been about to tell her something important. "Tiye told me. She heard it directly from Pharaoh."

"What is it?"

It couldn't be about Ishtar. Tiye would have told me herself if she had learned something. She wouldn't tell someone else and not me. But my heart seemed to still in my chest and I found myself holding my breath as I waited for Henutmire's news. It wouldn't be about Ishtar. It couldn't be.

And indeed it wasn't.

"Apparently my father has sent several letters asking to hear from me." Henutmire leaned towards my table as she spoke, keeping her voice low. "He has become concerned the messages he receives don't sound like me, and he is demanding Pharaoh provide proof I still live."

"You mean the messages the scribe sends for you?"

Henutmire nodded.

"No doubt he rewrites them to his own satisfaction," she said. "I have him write to my father twice every season, and he always seems to take a very long time to transcribe what I tell him."

Pentau had done the same when I asked him for a letter to my father, and he became incensed when I asked him to read it back. I suspected he had embellished his letter, but had no way of proving it. I had only the word of Tiye's maid who said the scribe's messages would always reflect favourably on my life here.

"Has Pharaoh made any reply to your father?" I asked.

"Tiye said he had a message sent after the first letter arrived, assuring my father of my safety. But my father has continued to send further letters, three in total now, I believe, and Pharaoh is furious. He has told Tiye he will not reply again."

"What do you think he will do?"

I wasn't sure whether I meant Pharaoh or her father. Henutmire shrugged.

"Father can be very determined when he has made up his mind about something," she said. "If he is questioning my safety, I don't believe he will let the matter drop. He will keep writing to Pharaoh until he receives a reply that satisfies him."

Would my father do such a thing? Would he risk the alliance for news of the daughter he had willingly sent away?

"If Pharaoh is angered..." My voice trailed away as I realised I wasn't sure what I could safely say. Tiye knew the truth of the missing women. If that had something to do with the business the Ornaments wouldn't discuss in front of me, then Henutmire undoubtedly knew it too. Surely she must recognise the danger in angering Pharaoh.

"Your father must love you very much," I said instead.

"It gives me much comfort," Henutmire replied. "I was very angry with him, you understand, when he first sent me here. I couldn't understand how he could do such a thing."

"Is your father a nobleman?" She was Egyptian born, but that was all I knew of her background. Her father couldn't be a king, but he was probably either a noble or a relative of Pharaoh.

"Yes, but my family is considered somewhat controversial," she said.

I waited for her to explain. She seemed to hesitate, perhaps wondering whether she really wanted to tell me.

"Many years ago, my ancestors ruled Upper Egypt. More than four hundred years ago. My father is a direct descendant of the very last pharaoh of that time."

"So you are a princess?"

Henutmire's mouth twisted as she pondered this.

"Of sorts, I suppose," she said. "I have never thought of it like that before. It matters little, though. There are many women here who are real princesses. I would not embarrass myself by making such a claim in their presence."

She gave me a nod, which I assumed was an acknowledgement of my own status. She was correct that it didn't matter whether she was a princess or not. Here the only division that mattered was between Ornament and servant. There was some distinction of status amongst the Ornaments from what

I had observed, but it was about seniority in terms of how long they had been here, and nothing to do with their background.

After all, Tiye was considered the Top Ornament and she was no princess. Her mother had been no more than a lady's maid — a servant, albeit to the queen. And yet Tiye rose to be Top Ornament and had been unchallenged ever since.

Well, that might change yet. I had told Ahmose I wanted to be powerful enough to be feared by Pharaoh. That would mean I was feared by others as well. The relationships I had built since I arrived here would likely shatter. The realisation saddened me, but I hardened my heart. I would do whatever I must to secure justice for Ishtar. If that meant my tenuous friendship with Tiye or Henutmire was destroyed, then so be it.

CHAPTER 26

$\mathcal{I}$ lay awake for a long time that night. The air in my bedchamber was stifling with the windows closed to keep out the insects. I tossed and turned, but couldn't get comfortable. Sweat dotted my forehead and my nightgown felt damp. Eventually, I rose and pulled on the first gown I found in my clothing chest. I couldn't bear to spend another moment tossing in bed.

No doubt everyone else would already be asleep. I wouldn't wake them. I would slip out, take a quick walk, and be back before anyone noticed I was gone. Ettu would fuss about me going alone, but Khaemmalu was out there and he wouldn't let harm come to me.

If there was any danger to the women in our Palace — and there was no certainty of that, given what we knew — then all I had to do was make my way through the hallways as quickly as possible. It must be well after midnight and anyone I encountered this late would probably be busy with their own tasks.

But when I tiptoed out to the sitting chamber, I found a lamp turned down low, and Ettu and Sehener immersed in a quiet conversation.

"My lady," Ettu said, giving me a startled look. "Are you unwell?"

"Can't sleep," I said. "I am going for a walk."

"And you intend to go alone?" She frowned at me, but I waved away her protest. Despite my inability to sleep, I was weary and not in the mood to argue with her.

"What I was intending is of no matter," I said. "Who will accompany me?"

There was no point trying to get out alone now. I didn't let myself think about the disappointment that I would, as always, have someone with me. There had been a tiny part of me that had anticipated the chance to see Khaemmalu without anyone to witness it, although I couldn't have said what I expected to happen that I wouldn't want someone to see.

"I will go with you." Sehener was already on her feet. "Ettu was just saying how tired she was."

"But not too tired to accompany my lady if she wishes me to," Ettu said and moved as if to get up.

I gestured for her to stay where she was.

"Sehener will come," I said. "Will you bar the door behind us?"

I had only been thinking of myself when I planned to slip out. I hadn't considered the danger to Tall if someone were to enter my unlocked chambers while I was out walking. At least if Ettu stayed, she could sleep on the couch while she waited for our return.

"Of course." Ettu frowned a little and I guessed she

wondered how I had intended to secure the door without waking anyone before I left.

As Sehener and I made our way through the Palace, I found myself waiting for her to speak. If it was Ettu, she would have some comment to make, or she would ask why I wanted to take a walk so late. But Sehener merely followed, walking a couple of paces behind me as was appropriate for a servant.

The air outside was still warm from the day and heady with fragrance, making my nose itch. I had thought it would be cooler by now. I tried not to sniffle as I set off down one of the paths. Sehener followed, still silent.

"Sehener, would you walk beside me?" I asked. "It is difficult to have a conversation with you like this."

She hurried to my side.

"I apologise, my lady," she said. "I didn't realise you would want to converse with me."

"Of course I do. It's pleasant to have someone to talk with while I walk."

"What would you like to discuss?" Sehener's voice was eager and I realised I'd probably never had a proper conversation with her. Not alone, at any rate.

"Tell me about yourself," I said. "How did you come to work here?"

"As you know, I was first employed by the Palace three years ago," she said. "I was eleven years old at that point. My mother went to the West when I was born and my father took a new wife while I was very young. He died when I was ten. His wife allowed me to continue living with her for a few months, but then she said she could no longer afford to support me. She intended to marry me to her cousin's son so he would have to pay my living expenses. I didn't like him. He had always been rather cruel to me. So I found a job and left her house. I came here after meeting one of the kitchen servants. She told me the Palace was always looking for staff and that I should talk to Panouk."

"Do you like your position?" I asked when she finally stopped for breath. I hadn't expected her to so readily share her story with me.

"Oh, I do," she said enthusiastically. "The work is neither onerous nor difficult. Especially now. Although I confess, my lady, I still don't understand what it is you want me to do all day."

"Just…" I waved my hand in the air, still having no further insight into what she was looking for than the last time she had asked. Merytre hadn't needed instructions when I invited her to move into my chambers. "Whatever you wish," I said eventually. "I will not ask much of you other than for you to attend me when I go out."

I waited for Sehener to reply, but she said nothing else. When I glanced over at her, she was frowning.

"Does this position displease you?" I asked. "Would you prefer to move back to the maids' dormitory? I wouldn't stop you if that's what you want."

"Oh no," she said quickly. "I hope you don't think me ungrateful. I'm just trying to understand your expectations. Most Ornaments select only a couple of favoured lady's maids to attend them during the day while the others are assigned to sewing or laundry or whatever. Some boast about how they are not required to do anything other than chat with their mistress, while others say they have a long list of chores to do every day. Ettu and Merytre have always been tight-lipped about their duties and would not tell us anything, so I am trying to ensure I have not misunderstood what you require of me."

"Sehener." I paused to sort through my thoughts. I wasn't sure whether she was afraid of upsetting me, or if she was just exceptionally diligent when it came to the requirements of her position. Surely I hadn't done anything that would make her fearful. "You can relax. If there is something I want you to do, I will tell you. You don't have to worry or to try to guess what I want."

"But that's the problem," she said earnestly. "You shouldn't have to tell me. A good lady's maid will anticipate her mistress's requirements and carry out her wishes before she is even aware of them herself. That is what I want to do."

Before I could reply, a nearby bush rustled. My heart leaped in a most unbecoming way. Such a rustle was usually Khaemmalu's way of telling me he was nearby. Indeed, a moment later, he stepped out and bowed to me.

"Good evening, Lady Kassaya," he said.

The moonlight was bright enough for me to see how his gaze quickly travelled from my head to my feet, before he fixed it firmly on my face. My cheeks heated and he surely must have noticed.

"Khaemmalu," I greeted him, then gestured towards Sehener. "This is Sehener."

He gave her a little bow.

"I know your name," he said, "although I don't believe I have ever seen your face before. You have never come out to the grounds at night, as far as I am aware."

"Oh." To my relief, Sehener blushed even harder than me. "I can't think how you would know of me. I am merely a lady's maid."

"I make it my business to know everyone." Khaemmalu's

voice was serious. "Especially those who attend Lady Kassaya."

"Of course." Sehener's laugh sounded like relief. "She is rather…"

"Exceptional," Khaemmalu said.

"Unusual," Sehener said at the same time.

Her laugh was a little more awkward this time.

"So I'm sure you will understand if I ask to walk with your mistress for a while?" Khaemmalu asked.

"Yes, yes. I will just…" Sehener gestured behind us, seemingly at nothing. "Walk behind you."

Khaemmalu gave her another little bow and indicated for me to continue walking. He fell in beside me.

"I think you quite bamboozled her," I said after a glance over my shoulder to make sure Sehener wouldn't hear. "I have never seen her so flustered."

"I suspect she hasn't met any of the guards before," he said. "And that is fortunate. She seems quite innocent and there are men here who would take advantage of that."

"Oh." I cast a sideways glance at him, trying not to let him catch me, and prayed he wouldn't notice my blush. "I thought all the guards would be…"

"Be what?" he asked when I didn't finish.

Like you, I thought, but I couldn't say it. I only shook my head.

"I don't know," I said.

"I think you do."

Startled, I looked straight at him to find him staring at me.

"You can be honest with me, Kassaya." His voice was low and intimate.

Flustered, I looked away, out into the darkness.

"Come with me." Khaemmalu stepped off the path and ducked behind a shrub.

I glanced back at Sehener who watched with evident curiosity. She gave me a small nod, then turned her back, signalling she saw nothing of what I did. I hesitated only a moment longer and prayed to Marduk I wouldn't regret this.

Taking a deep breath, I followed Khaemmalu into the shadows.

CHAPTER 27

The area behind the shrubs was shielded by the branches of a large tamarisk tree which provided a private nook of greenery. Only the barest hint of moonlight made its way through the leaves. Khaemmalu waited there for me, although all I could see of him was a dark shape. As I reached him, he leaned back against the trunk. I couldn't make out his eyes, but I could feel them boring into me.

"What are we doing here?" My voice was a little shaky and I was grateful the darkness hid my blush. Marduk, he would think I was afraid if he could see me right now.

"Talking," he said. "I believe you were about to tell me what you thought the guards would be like."

When I didn't reply, he peeled himself off the trunk and took two steps towards me. He was so close, I could feel his breath on my face, although I couldn't make out his features. His eyes were no more than dark pools.

"I already know the rest of your secrets," he said. "Why keep this one from me?"

"It's not a secret," I whispered.

His fingers grazed my hand. "Then why won't you tell me?"

"Because it's embarrassing."

His laugh was low and molten. My breath hitched.

"You need never be embarrassed with me," he said.

I couldn't think of a reply that neither sounded inane nor revealed far too much of my thoughts. When I didn't respond, Khaemmalu took a step back. The space between us seemed so vast now, even though I could have closed the gap with a single step. If I dared to.

"I heard the news about Sutem and Merytre," he said.

This, at least, was something I could discuss.

"I am very happy for them," I said. "This is not a—"

I stopped as I realised what I was about to say. This is not an easy place to find love. Had I said that, Khaemmalu might have taken it as an invitation. He might have thought I hinted I was open to an affair. With him. I expected him to ask what I had meant to say and I searched for an answer that would be less revealing. But although he must have noticed my unsaid words, he didn't question me.

"Sutem is very happy," he said instead. "We can all only wish for such happiness as he has found with Merytre."

Although his tone was as easy as ever, a tinge of envy seemed to underpin his words. He had told me three years had passed since his wife, Tabiry, disappeared. Was he lonely when he went home each day at dawn? But perhaps he didn't go home alone. Maybe he didn't even go home at all, but to someone else's house. A woman's. I knew only that he believed Tabiry to be dead and he no longer considered himself married. I didn't know he was actually alone.

Jealousy stirred within me at the thought of Khaemmalu with another woman, but that was ridiculous. I had no claim over him and, in truth, I could never be with him. Not with the threat of execution hanging over both of us. My stomach fluttered and I tried to push my jealousy aside. But it wasn't jealousy making my stomach feel so odd. It was probably the babe.

My son.

Khaemmalu didn't know I was with child. Or if he did, he had never mentioned it.

"I should go," I said, taking a hurried step back.

My sandal caught and I stumbled. Khaemmalu was swift to grab my arms before I could fall. This close to him, the heat from his body surged against me and did strange things to my insides. His hands lingered on my upper arms.

"I'm sorry if I have kept you too long from your walk," he said.

His eyes seemed to search my face for something, although I didn't dare let myself wonder what.

I stepped back, more carefully this time, and his hands released me. I regretted it immediately. I wanted to move forward, towards him, not away. I longed to lean into his warmth and put my hands on his chest and…

What was I thinking? There could never be anything between us. I carried Pharaoh's son in my belly. I was Pharaoh's property and Khaemmalu was charged with protecting me.

I was nothing more to him than a distraction during a long shift. No, that was unfair of me. I might not know Khaemmalu very well, but I didn't believe he was that kind of man. But what kind of man was he to risk execution for the merest brush of a hand?

I fled without another word. Back out to the safety of the

moonlight and the path and Sehener waiting for me. She turned at the sound of my footsteps.

"My lady?" she asked. "Are you well?"

I stopped in front of her and smoothed my wig, although I didn't know why I did such a thing. It wasn't like Khaemmalu had touched me there.

"Perfectly," I said. "We should continue our walk."

She kept pace beside me without further question. If it was Ettu, she would have asked what had occurred with Khaemmalu to send me rushing out of the shrubbery like that. But if Sehener was curious, she held her tongue.

I was thankful she didn't ask, because I wasn't sure I knew myself what had just happened between us. If the situation had been different — if I wasn't an Ornament and forbidden from the hands of anyone but Pharaoh — I might have thought Khaemmalu was interested in me. That perhaps he wanted to kiss me. But he knew as well as I did what the punishment for such an offence would be. He wouldn't dare it.

We walked for only a short while longer before I told Sehener I was tired and we turned back to retrace our steps. If Khaemmalu was still nearby, I saw no sign of him, or indeed of any other guard.

It was only as we approached the Palace entrance that I let myself feel the disappointment of walking away from the possibility of whatever might have occurred with Khaemmalu, even though I knew there was no other option.

Back in my bed, I found myself no more able to sleep than before my walk, only this time, it was thoughts of Khaemmalu keeping me awake. The huskiness in his voice as he asked what I had thought the guards would be like. The warmth of his hand as it grazed mine. The way the air between us seemed to crackle. It was a long time before I fell asleep.

The next morning, my head was fuzzy and I could hardly keep my eyes open. I lay on the couch for a while, but I couldn't sleep and doing nothing only made me feel worse, so I decided to visit Tiye. As Ettu walked me to Tiye's chambers a short while later, I wondered whether this was a mistake.

Tiye was not the easiest person to talk to since it often seemed her words could be interpreted in more than one way. I hadn't seen her since she told me there was no certainty of retirement to a villa once my childbearing years were over. I felt like that conversation wasn't finished, but I didn't know how to pursue it. But I also couldn't bear to be in my chambers this morning, it was already too hot to walk outside, and I didn't know what else to do with myself.

When I arrived, Tiye was standing at a window.

"Good morning," she said, sounding reasonably cheerful.

If she remembered our last conversation, she didn't seem to feel any awkwardness about it. How irritating that she was never anything but confident.

"Do you ever go out or do you just stand at the window?" I asked, somewhat grumpily as I sat down without waiting for an invitation.

Tiye turned to give me an appraising stare.

"That was unusually ill-tempered for you," she said.

"Perhaps you have forgotten my sister is still missing and presumed dead."

I regretted my words as soon as they were said. Ishtar had nothing to do with my mood today.

"I'm sorry," I started, but Tiye waved away my apology.

"Don't," she said. "You owe me neither apology nor explanation."

"I didn't sleep well," I said, feeling like I should explain regardless.

Tiye shot me a look that said she knew it wasn't the whole truth as she came to sit on the couch in front of me. She took a long time to smooth her skirt over her knees, something I recognised by now as a way of giving her time to think about what she intended to say. I waited, and indeed her next words confirmed she had chosen them carefully.

"I'm not sure you really understand the situation here," she began.

"I suspect I know more than you think."

I held her gaze, noting how her eyes widened slightly at my response. She was adept at not revealing her thoughts, but the longer I knew her, the more I was learning the slight ways she revealed herself.

"What is it you think you know?" she asked.

"When you decide to be frank with me, I will tell you what I know," I said. "Until then, I suppose we will each keep our own counsel."

She glanced away for a moment, smoothing her skirt again. I had made her uncomfortable. The more we edged around speaking the truth, the more certainty I had that there was something I didn't know yet. Whether it was about the missing women, or the eventual fates of every Ornament, or something else entirely, I couldn't begin to imagine. I pressed my lips together, resolving not to demand she tell me everything. Given my lack of sleep and the fuzziness of my mind, this was probably not an ideal moment to press her for details.

"That is as it may be," Tiye said, and any chance of the truth, in this conversation at least, was gone. "Do you play *senet*?"

She nodded to a table which bore a game board. Two chairs drawn up to the table suggested she had played with someone recently.

"I am passingly familiar with the game," I said. "But I haven't yet had the chance to learn."

"Come then. I will teach you."

We moved to the little table and she explained the rules. I already knew it was a game of strategy, and it sounded far too complicated for my sleep-deprived brain to make sense of.

Her *senet* board looked much more valuable than the one Ahmose and Tall played on. Both boards were set into the top of the box in which the playing pieces were stored, but where Ahmose's board was a wooden sheet painted with the *senet* grid, Tiye's was made of different kinds of wood cunningly slotted together. Ahmose's playing pieces were plain, with a different wood for each player. Tiye's had sparkling gems set into their tops, yellow for one player and green for the other.

She explained the rules and we began to play. We didn't speak much at first, other than her explanations when I made the wrong move.

"This is a very fine board," I said as I waited for her next move.

"A gift from Pharaoh." Tiye's voice was absent, as if her focus was entirely on the game.

Gone was any beauty in the board and now all I could see was a set gifted by hands stained with murder. Tiye moved her playing piece and sat back in her chair. She nodded at me to take my turn.

"He enjoys *senet*," she said. "If he desires you to play against him, you should ensure you let him win."

I glanced up from the board, my hand hesitating over the piece I had been about to move.

"Not that I think that will be any problem for you," she observed, arching her eyebrows.

It was a clear indication my move was a poor choice, but I couldn't see any other option available to me, so I did it anyway, then shrugged at her.

"I've heard Weren is still sniffing around," she said, her hand hesitating over a playing piece before she changed her mind and moved another. "He remains convinced someone in the Palace is using magic."

Since she hadn't mentioned the butler's search for evidence of magic use again recently, I had assumed he gave up.

"Haven't all the odd things stopped?" I asked. "I haven't heard of anything else since the ceremony for Kia."

There had been a number of strange occurrences before that, which folk blamed on Kia's spirit being unsettled after her sudden and tragic drowning the day we sailed with Pharaoh. Food spoiling faster than it should have, a flock of hens that suddenly died overnight, items disappearing, including the chest containing the things I bought with me from Babylon. It mysteriously reappeared after Kia's farewell and although I was never quite convinced it could really be her spirit doing such things, I was thankful to have the chest back.

Lost in my thoughts, I didn't realise Tiye hadn't responded. She stared at the game, but the look on her face suggested she wasn't really seeing it.

"Tiye?" I asked. "Are you well?"

"Of course," she said. "Your turn."

"I don't know what my next move should be."

I slid a playing piece across to the next square, then realised my error. I had given Tiye a clear path to win. She frowned.

"Your lack of strategy baffles me," she said. "I think you comprehend far more than you let on, but you appear to have no clear plan for how to proceed."

She looked me right in the eyes and I understood we weren't talking about the game now.

"I think you have your own plan." The "business" the women wouldn't discuss in front of me. "So I'm not sure why my plan, or lack of, bothers you."

"You could be dangerous, I think." Tiye returned her gaze to the board and moved her final playing piece. "I win."

"Dangerous? Me?"

She swept the playing pieces into her palm and dropped them in the drawer beneath the board.

"As I said, you *appear* to have no plan," she said. "You give the impression of innocence and ignorance. What I can't figure out is how true that is."

"If you would just speak plainly, we could establish whether we both have the same aims," I said. "I tire of talking in riddles."

Tiye let out a long breath. She seemed to be coming to a decision and my heart pounded in anticipation. This was it. She was finally going to tell me whatever it was she had been hiding.

"Kassaya, there are things you don't know about this place." Tiye stopped, as if she was still undecided how much to tell me.

"As you already said, I know more than you think," I said. "But go on."

"Pharaoh likes to see a woman in pain." She spoke quickly as if wanting to get the words out before she could change her mind. "It excites him. Makes him feel powerful."

This was nothing I hadn't already guessed, but I baulked at hearing it said so baldly.

"He doesn't already feel powerful enough?" I kept my tone casual and tried to pretend I was at ease with the conversation. "Being king of one of the most wealthy countries in the world? And there's the whole living god thing."

My words were deliberately indifferent, and I thought she would chastise me, but her face showed she took me more seriously than I expected. That there was more to it than I had guessed. That the truth was impossibly dark and terrible.

"No," she said. "It is not enough for him. Sometimes in order to bed a woman, he needs her to…"

Her voice trailed away. I waited.

"He needs her to think she might not survive," she said at last.

The chamber around us seemed to fade away. I focussed all my attention on Tiye and tried not to let myself feel her words. If I felt them, I'd fall apart, and I couldn't do that here.

"So he chokes you." I forced it out, trying not to let her see how her words had affected me.

She looked at me steadily.

"Yes," she said. "And a wise woman will let him do it."

"What is wise about letting him almost kill you?"

"Because that is what he likes. If you struggle too much and he has to hold you down, he… loses focus. He can't perform. And that makes him angry."

"He likes to choke you, but only as long as you don't struggle?"

Had Ishtar struggled? Hilde didn't. She told me she froze. She probably didn't know that might have saved her life.

Tiye shrugged and didn't answer.

"How many times has he done that to you?" I asked.

She frowned a little and flicked her hand at me, as if trying to wave away the question.

"Enough," she said.

"Enough times?" I asked. "Enough for what?"

Or maybe she meant enough of my questions.

"Enough for him to know I won't struggle," she said. "Enough for him to know he has absolute power over me."

"Absolute power? You mean, you let him think he could kill you and you wouldn't even try to defend yourself?"

She looked at me for a long moment.

"I have told you before that you're naive," she said. "This is how the world works, Kassaya. Powerful men control our lives. The only thing we control is the decision of whether to submit or to fight."

"I would fight," I said. "Every time."

"And that is how you would end up dead."

"Are you saying that's what happens to the women who go missing? They fight back and he kills them?"

She looked away.

"Tiye, tell me the truth. Is that what happened to Ishtar? She fought back against Pharaoh when he tried to choke her?"

She gave a heavy sigh and her gaze wandered around the chamber, as if she tried to avoid meeting my eyes. At last, she looked at me.

"Yes," she said. "That is exactly what I think happened to your sister."

CHAPTER 29

$\mathcal{I}$ barely remembered leaving Tiye's chambers. Her admission had shocked me. I already knew Pharaoh was probably responsible for Ishtar's disappearance, but to hear Tiye say in such certain terms exactly what might have happened badly unsettled me. And to know why he did such a thing. I would never be able to say I understood it, but now at least I knew what had probably happened.

Ishtar was dead. There could be no doubt about it. She must have fought back. Surely any woman would. Or, rather, any woman other than Tiye who somehow knew what a mistake that would be.

The only question was whether Ishtar's body would ever be found. We knew it was probably Pharaoh's captain and his second who disposed of the bodies. They had made a mistake when they left a body at the quarry where it could be found. They surely wouldn't make the same mistake again. However they disposed of my sister's body, they would have been careful to ensure nobody would stumble over her. And I would have to write to my father. I no longer had any excuse not to.

"My lady?"

I didn't notice Ettu until she shook me by the shoulders.

"My lady!" she said.

I wiped my wet cheeks, only just now realising I was crying.

"Whatever happened in there?" Ettu asked. "You burst out of Lady Tiye's chambers as if a demon was chasing after you."

"I think one was."

I hardly knew what I was saying. I opened my mouth and words came out. Did they even make any sense? I didn't know and I didn't care.

"A demon chased you out of Lady Tiye's chambers?" Ettu asked.

When I didn't respond, she took me by the arm and pulled me down the hallway.

"Come on," she said. "We need to get you back to your chambers. I'm sure you don't want anyone seeing you in such a state."

Was this what the scaled priestess was trying to warn me about? *They will draw you in. Leave while you can. You do not want to be involved with what is coming.*

"I have to find her," I said, trying to shake off Ettu's hand. "The priestess. The one who talks to the flowers. They spoke to me once. They told me something important. I just can't remember what."

Ettu steered me along the hallway and around the corner.

"Merytre," she called as we reached my chambers. "Let us in. Quickly."

The soft click of the bar. The door swung open. I couldn't

make my feet move until Ettu pushed me inside. Merytre quickly closed the door behind us.

"What in Amun's name happened?" she asked Ettu.

Ettu pushed me towards a couch. My sandal caught on a rug, but both Ettu and Merytre were there to grab my arms before I fell.

"Ahmose," Ettu called. "It is like after the sailing accident. She is talking nonsense and her skin is cold."

Someone pushed me down into a chair. Ahmose came to peer intently at my face. This close, I could see the creases around her eyes, the deep lines on either side of her mouth. Her skin was leathery, weathered by the sun. I had never noticed that before.

"I will fetch my herbs," Ahmose said. "Merytre, I need hot water."

Someone draped a blanket over me and tucked it around my body. Its warmth was a welcome haven as I leaned back against the couch. The chamber went dark and some time passed before I realised it was because I had closed my eyes. I stirred only when Ahmose tapped my arm.

"My lady," she said. "Sit up. I need you to drink this."

"Go away," I muttered, or that was what I tried to say at any rate.

I had to find the seer. She obviously knew something and I would make her tell me what it was. I tried to get up, but then Ettu was there pushing me back onto the couch.

"You must stay there until you come to your senses," she said, tucking the blanket around me again. "Now, Ahmose has made you a nice hot brew, which you are going to drink. You will feel much better after that."

My limbs went weak and I didn't have the strength to argue with her. Ahmose pressed a mug into my hand and wrapped my cold fingers around it. Its warmth seeped into my hand. When did I get so cold? I couldn't remember ever being anything but cold. Why had I thought it was so hot lately?

"My lady, you must drink it." Ettu's voice was firm. "Come on, let me help you hold it to your mouth. Like that. Take a sip. Now another."

The heat from Ahmose's brew spread through my body. I closed my eyes, my focus following the warm trail as it trickled down my throat and into my belly. The heat spread through my arms and my legs, even all the way down to my frozen toes.

The mug was no longer in my hands. Someone had taken it, or I had dropped it. I supposed that meant it was empty. It didn't matter. Its warmth was inside me, unfurling through me the way a tree's roots wove through the ground beneath it. A nearby conversation penetrated the fog surrounding me.

"Let her rest. She will come back to herself soon enough. The brew was well dosed."

"Whatever happened?"

"I have no idea. She was like that when she came out of Lady Tiye's chambers."

"Lady Tiye must have said something that shocked her."

"Do you think Lady Tiye told her something new about what happened to Lady Ishtar?"

"Maybe. Whatever was said must be terrible. I have never seen her like this before."

"She is worse than she was after the sailing accident."

"Give her time. The herbs will work quickly and once she is rested, she will recover."

"Should we send for the physician?"

"I don't think she would want anyone else to see her like this."

"Leave her be. I am perfectly well equipped to manage such a situation."

The voices faded away and if anything else was said, I missed it.

When I woke, the chamber was dark, lit only by a single lamp turned down low. I still sat on the couch, swaddled in blankets, a low stool propped under my feet. I must have made some noise because Ettu was suddenly crouched in front of me.

"My lady?" she asked. "Are you awake?"

I blinked at her, trying to remember how to speak.

"My lady?" She shook my arm. "Can you hear me?"

"Yes," I finally managed. "I hear you."

"Oh, thank Marduk. I was starting to think you had woken insensible. How do you feel? Do you need anything? There is more of Ahmose's brew. Let me fetch you some."

She hurried away, leaving me sitting there, trying to make sense of her rapid stream of words. Ettu pressed a mug into my hands and I barely noticed myself move as I drank from it. The brew was little more than lukewarm, but it did help me feel more like myself.

"How long did I sleep?" I asked.

"Hours. It must be nearly dawn."

"Have you been sitting up all night?" Her eyes were large in a too pale face. Her face was thinner than it used to be. She had lost weight since Half was injured. I hadn't noticed before.

"Merytre sat with you for a while. Ahmose said you should be well by the time you woke, but we wanted to be sure. You were quite irrational. Something about flowers talking to you."

I only dimly remembered what happened between the time I left Tiye's chambers and when I woke on the couch, but I could still feel the overwhelming panic. The tightness of my chest and how I suddenly couldn't breathe. The way my thoughts tangled and the only thing I was sure of was that the flowers had told me something important which I had forgotten. That I'd never be able to breathe again unless I remembered what they told me.

"I don't know what I said." She would only be more concerned if she knew the truth.

Ettu gave me a look that said she didn't believe me, but she let the matter drop. She took the mug from my hands and set it on a table.

"You should go back to sleep," she said. "Do you want to go to your bedchamber?"

"No, I'll stay here." Indeed, Ahmose's brew had done its job again, spreading its warmth through my body. I was cozy under the blanket and really felt too lazy to move. "Go to bed. You don't need to stay with me."

Ettu hesitated, but then she yawned and that seemed to decide her.

"If you're sure," she said, already on her way to the door.

I rested my head against the back of the couch and didn't bother to reply. When I next woke, the sun was up and so was everyone else. Ettu and Merytre stood in the far corner of the sitting chamber, talking quietly. Ahmose was in her favourite chair, her feet propped up on a footstool. Tall stood beside the window.

I thought nobody had noticed I was awake, but when my gaze returned to Ahmose, she was watching me.

"Feeling better?" she asked.

Her question drew Ettu and Merytre's attention. Tall was the only one who didn't seem to notice, still absorbed in whatever he could see outside.

"Much better," I said. "Your brew helped. What was in it?"

"My own concoction," Ahmose said. "It contains a number of herbs, including juniper to ease the chest muscles, liquorice to soothe the internal organs, and a very small amount of poppy to calm the mind and help you breathe more easily. That was the last of my poppy, so I will need to get more today."

"I can come with you," Merytre offered. "Just let me know when you want to go."

Ahmose gave her a nod and any further conversation was halted by a knock at the door.

"That should be breakfast," Ettu said.

Tall hurried off to the men's bedchamber while Merytre waited at the sitting chamber door, ready to let in the kitchen servants. I pitied Tall for being confined yet again to his bedchamber. My maids would arrive soon and it would be a couple of hours, at least, before they left. Tall probably wouldn't even have the chance to break his fast until after that.

It was only later as my maids bathed me that I realised I hadn't even told anyone what I had learned.

CHAPTER 30

After my maids finally finished dressing me, I went back out to the sitting chamber. I wouldn't go to see Tiye today. I couldn't. Not after what she told me. I wouldn't be able to look her in the eyes without imagining her being pinned to a bed by her throat and all because Pharaoh liked to see a woman unable to breathe.

"You were very distressed yesterday," Ettu said as she settled herself on a nearby couch. "You haven't yet told us what Lady Tiye said to upset you like that."

How could I possibly tell them such an awful thing? I cast my gaze around the sitting chamber, trying to find a reason not to answer. Tall and Sehener sat together. Interesting the way they seemed to have formed an instant bond, and it had helped Tall break through his inability to speak in Egyptian. He seemed happier now. He spent less of his day sleeping and more of it in the sitting chamber with the rest of us. It pleased me that he had a friend here, even in Half's absence.

Ettu was on the couch she usually shared with Half. By some unspoken agreement, nobody ever sat in his usual place.

Maybe it was a way of acknowledging we expected him to return. Ahmose and Merytre each sat in single chairs. Merytre had already retrieved her stitching from where she had left it hanging over the arm, although she set it in her lap while she waited for me to speak.

Haltingly, I told them what Tiye had revealed. The expressions on their faces echoed the horror that still reverberated through me. When I finished, Ettu was the first to speak.

"Well," she said briskly. "We already knew Pharaoh was responsible. This just confirms it."

"But it's worse than we thought," Merytre said. "We thought…"

Her voice trailed away and I could only guess at what she didn't want to say. We thought he killed because he couldn't help himself. That he went into a rage and couldn't control himself. We never thought it might be because he gained pleasure from it. Because sometimes it was the only way he could bed a woman. I wasn't sure that one was necessarily any worse than the other. They were both terrible.

"I suppose…" Sehener's voice trailed away and we all looked at her as we waited for her to finish. "I suppose Lady Ishtar must have fought him."

"I should have made her leave." The words came out of my mouth automatically. I was so used to thinking like that, I barely even noticed. It was only after I said it that I realised there was no point thinking in such a way. Ishtar was gone and there was no way to change that. The only thing I could do now was find a way to stop it from happening to any other woman. And I had a plan for that.

"She wouldn't have left," Ettu pointed out. "Where would she have gone anyway? So the only question now is what my lady intends to do about it."

I willed myself to meet her gaze and not look at Ahmose. Even so much as a glance at the old woman would give me away. Ettu would know there was something I hadn't told them.

"I don't see there is anything I can do," I said. "We have discussed this before. I cannot go to the administrators or the police chief."

"I find it hard to believe you don't intend to do anything," Ettu said.

Why did everyone think I would do something? What had I done to make them think me the kind of person who would even try?

"Pharaoh is above the law," I said. "That is what everyone keeps telling me."

Ettu harrumphed, a noise that said clearly she knew I was lying. Sehener's gaze travelled between Ettu and me, and although she said nothing, I saw how she tracked every sign. She was like Ettu, letting nothing slip past her. She was just a little more reluctant to speak up.

"I suppose," Merytre started. She stopped, cleared her throat, looked up at the ceiling.

"Go on then," Ettu said.

"I suppose it would take a plan," Merytre said. "A well thought out one."

"Do you understand what you are suggesting?" Ahmose asked her. "How it would be viewed if anyone else heard you?"

"Treason." Merytre's voice was calm.

"Probably heresy as well," Sehener added.

Ahmose gave no sign of whether she agreed with their assessment, only continued to study Merytre with the same calm look she used for everything.

"You should not discuss such a thing," I said, giving both Merytre and Sehener a firm look. "Not even here."

"Who here will judge me?" Merytre asked. "We who know the truth of what has happened."

"We who recognise the injustice of living in a world where a man can claim to be a god," Ettu added.

"We who see the terrible grief you are enduring," Sehener said.

"Me!" Tall said.

"Yes," Sehener said to him. "You see it, too." She turned back to me. "We all see it, my lady. If you have a plan to avenge Lady Ishtar, we will help you."

"Perhaps," Ahmose said, her tone mild enough that it gave no hint of what she was about to say, "the way you can help is by pretending you know nothing."

"Aha," Ettu said. "So there is a plan. And yet you won't share it with us." She gave me a reproachful look. "Have we not done enough to secure your trust? Have I not done enough? We have kept every secret you have shared with us. You told us yourself Lady Tiye said no information leaves your chambers. That in itself is proof of our loyalty. If anyone could uncover the most elusive details, it would be her. Yet even she has failed."

"It is not that I don't trust you," I said. "But the stakes are too high. If it is uncovered, it would mean death for everyone involved."

My own words made me pause. I knew the punishment for both treason and heresy would be execution. It could hardly be anything less. But I hadn't thought about what it would mean for me personally.

Would I be burnt alive? Beheaded? Whatever my fate if my fledgling plan were revealed, it would certainly be excruciating. Only the most horrific punishment would be reserved for such a crime. And despite what the Egyptians believed about the necessity of preserving the body after death, that surely wouldn't be granted to someone convicted of treason or heresy. Their final and greatest punishment would be eternal death.

Was it worth it? The possibility of not only death, but an incredibly painful one. If my plan was uncovered before my babe was born, would they allow me to give birth before they carried out my sentence? If my son was already delivered, would my punishment be extended to him too? Would being the son of Pharaoh be enough to save him from his mother's crimes?

Was that the choice I had to make? Justice for Ishtar, and for every woman Pharaoh had killed, or might yet kill, weighed against the life of my son?

One life versus many.

The answer should be easy.

It wasn't.

CHAPTER 31

"I am going for a walk," I said, getting to my feet.

I didn't have the answers they wanted and I couldn't bear to sit here any longer while they looked at me with such dismay. Even Tall's face said I had disappointed him. They wanted to hear I had a plan, and now they not only knew I did, but that I wouldn't share it with them.

"I will come with you," Ettu said quickly.

I was tempted to say I would take Merytre, because she would be less likely to continue her interrogation in private, but Ettu would be offended and I would only have to make it up to her later.

"Very well," I said instead.

Tall slipped away while we left and I didn't miss the way Sehener's gaze followed him as he left the chamber. Merytre came to bar the door behind us. She and Ettu seemed to exchange a significant look before the door closed. I sighed inwardly. So it was not only me who expected the discussion to continue.

Ettu was blessedly silent as we made our way down the

three flights of stairs to the ground level. I knew she wouldn't risk saying anything where we might be overheard. She would at least have the sense to hold her tongue until we were out in the gardens.

I greeted Khaemope and Karpusa as we exited the front doors.

"My lady," one of them said with a solemn nod.

I still wasn't quite sure which was which, and enough time had passed since I first met them that I felt I couldn't ask.

Ettu kept pace with me, although, to my surprise, she still held her tongue. Perhaps she was waiting for me to offer something. A glimpse into my plans. A better explanation of why I was keeping secrets.

The sun was only midway to its peak, but already the air was uncomfortably hot. I chose a path that led a winding circuit amongst the trees in the hope it would be cooler within their shade. But then I realised my mistake.

I should have taken the route through the flower beds. They were hidden from me as we passed between the trees. What if the seer with the scaled face was there? I might miss her. I hadn't seen her again since that first day, except in the dream where she told me to leave while I could. Or maybe it wasn't a dream. I was no longer sure. The only thing I was certain of was that she knew something and I had to find out what it was.

"Are you looking for something?" Ettu asked, as observant as ever, although her tone was chilly. She wanted me to know she was still upset.

As I debated how to answer, she let out a little huff and dropped back to walk behind me. It was a clear message that if I didn't trust her, she wouldn't be anything more than a servant to me.

"Walk with me, Ettu," I said. "I wasn't refusing to answer. I was just trying to figure out how to explain."

She returned to my side, although her shoulders were still stiff and she didn't speak.

"I had this dream," I started.

I wasn't yet sure whether I would tell her I had dreamed about the seer, or about the narcissus that protected me and once spoke to me, or about the lions that seemed to be everywhere. We kept walking while I tried to find the right words. The path turned and twisted between the trees. As we came around a bend shielded by the gnarled trunk of a large acacia, I saw her.

The seer stood in the middle of the path. She seemed to be doing nothing other than waiting. For me, I assumed. Her shoulders were hunched in the manner of an old woman who can no longer straighten her back. The shawl draped over her head hung low, obscuring her face. I didn't need to see the scales to know it was the woman I had previously encountered in the gardens. The one who told me I should leave while I could.

"It's you," I said coming to an abrupt halt. Ettu walked another pace or two before noticing I had stopped.

My cheeks heated as I realised the foolishness of my words, but if the seer thought me odd, she gave no sign of it.

"It is I," she agreed. "You were looking for me and now you have found me."

"How did you know I was looking for you?"

I had barely acknowledged it even to myself. She must have known before I did or she couldn't have been here ahead of me. The seer cocked her head to the side and although the shawl shielded her eyes, I felt she studied me.

What did she see when she looked at me? Did she see only

what others did, the Babylonian princess, now an Ornament of Pharaoh, perfectly presented thanks to my maids, if lacking the elegance of other women? Or did she see inside me to where I nursed my anger and resentment and plans of revenge? The seer didn't speak, only waited for me to continue.

"You told me to leave," I said. "Tell me why."

"A lion's roar will shatter secrets." Her tone was conversational, giving no hint as to whether she considered her words to be important.

Shocked at her mention of lions, I took a step back. My sandal caught on the path's edge and I stumbled. My cheeks, already hot, burned even more at this demonstration of my inelegance.

It wasn't just the seer I had dreamed of. I dreamed of lions as well, over and over. Stalking me. Following me through the gardens. Even during the day, it seemed lions surrounded me. The little lioness offering from Ineni to Kia. The changing of the seasons ceremony for Isis and Nephthys, during which a priestess wearing a lioness's mask prowled around us. Merytre's wall hanging of the lioness goddess, completed some weeks ago and hung on the wall in her old bedchamber. I avoided looking at it when I passed her chamber and hadn't checked to see if she had taken it to Sutem's house. There were lions everywhere.

"I don't understand what that means," I said, when I had finally gathered myself enough to speak.

The seer only looked at me. Or at least I thought she did. With the shawl hanging so low over her face, I couldn't see precisely where she looked, but I felt her stare. It burned almost as hot as my cheeks still did.

"Don't you?" she asked.

Ettu cleared her throat as if she was about to speak. I glanced at her for a moment and when I looked back, the seer was gone.

"Wait!" I called.

But if the seer heard me, she made no reply. Nor did she return.

CHAPTER 32

*J*felt out of sorts for the rest of the day. The seer's words had disturbed me. I tried to tell myself they mightn't mean anything. A lion's roar will shatter secrets? It was too vague, too generic to be meaningful. It was probably just one of those things a seer said to sound mysterious. She didn't need to actually know anything to recognise that secrets abounded in a place like this. Anywhere there were people, there were secrets. It meant nothing.

But I couldn't shake the uneasiness. If it was indeed just a vague, mysterious-sounding statement, why did she mention a lion? She could have chosen any other animal. A dog's bark. A hippopotamus's bellow. An eagle's cry. But she chose a lion.

When I went to bed that night, I tossed and turned for what felt like hours. The air in my bedchamber was too hot, leaving my skin damp with sweat, and I couldn't get comfortable. Eventually, I got up and flung open the shutters. The biting insects were preferable to the stifling air.

The moon was high and the night air refreshing. I breathed deeply, feeling my tension ease. It was the seer's fault

I felt so unsettled. Talking with her had disturbed me more than I realised. I wouldn't seek her out again.

Down in the grounds, I caught a glimpse of someone walking. From this distance, I couldn't make out the identity of the shadowy figure. It could be an Ornament, or perhaps a maid. Maybe even one of the guards making his rounds of the gardens.

I pulled on a gown and a wig, refusing to let myself think about who I hoped it might be. Whoever I had seen would be gone by the time I got out there anyway. It didn't matter who it was. But the air outside was cooler than my bedchamber and a walk might ease my discomfort enough to let me sleep. That was what I told myself anyway.

The sitting chamber was all in darkness and it seemed everyone else was in bed. I had expected one of the others to still be up. There was always someone still awake when I decided on a late night walk. I weighed having to wake someone against the risk of leaving the door unbarred if I went out alone.

Say someone came to my chambers and tried the door, not expecting to find it unbarred. But when the door opened, well, maybe they came inside and snooped around. Maybe they found Tall in his bedchamber. Or maybe they took Ettu, or Sehener, or even Ahmose. Merytre had said there were stories of women taken from their chambers at night. Perhaps I shouldn't go.

Before I could decide what to do, Sehener came in, wearing a linen nightgown and no wig. Perhaps I had disturbed her when I came out here.

"Oh," she said on finding me standing there. "I thought you went to bed."

She passed one hand over her head, as if embarrassed at being seen without a wig.

"I did," I said.

"I came to get a drink." She went to the table where there was always an assortment of wine, beer and melon juice. "Can I pour you something?"

I shook my head. Sehener downed her drink quickly, watching me as she did.

"Do you need something?" she asked, setting down her mug.

"No."

"I suppose I'm wondering why you're just standing there."

"I was thinking of taking a walk."

"Let me get dressed. I will only be a moment." She was already on her way back to her bedchamber.

"You don't need to come," I said.

"You can hardly go alone." She stopped in the doorway. "It isn't safe. Ettu was most strident when she told me none of us should go anywhere by ourselves."

"I don't believe the danger is in this palace."

She studied me, and I saw her indecision between duty and the desire to go back to sleep. If Ettu had been the one to catch me, she would insist on coming. I was pleased it was Sehener.

"Perhaps you could wait here," I said. "I was worried about leaving the door unbarred. If you slept on a couch, I could wake you when I get back."

Sehener glanced towards the hallway leading to the bedchambers, as if wondering whether Ettu might be listening. She restrained a yawn, which seemed to decide her.

"Very well," she said. "I will be right here on the couch."

I heard the bar slip into place behind me as I left. This late, the Palace was quiet, and I passed only the occasional servant or runner boy. As I made my way down the stairs, another Ornament was on her way up. She eyed me as we approached each other, her haughty stare exactly the same as when I met her at Kia's farewell ceremony. Her black skin glistened in the torch light.

"Amanitore," I greeted her, hoping I had her name right.

She looked me up and down, and at first I thought she didn't intend to reply.

"Kassaya, isn't it?" she said at last. "The Babylonian?"

Her mouth twisted a little, as if she intended it as an insult.

"That is correct." I kept my tone easy, determined to be polite even if she wasn't. With the number of secrets I kept, I didn't want to give anyone a reason to look too hard at me.

"I heard about the other Babylonian," she said. "Your sister. I am sorry."

Her tone didn't soften, leaving me to conclude she wasn't sorry at all.

"Thank you," I said. "I'm still hopeful she will be found safe."

Even as the words left my mouth, I knew I was lying. I had no hope left. Not after so many days. Not after how much I knew.

"Yet you still wander the Palace alone at night?" Amanitore's stare burned into me. "A sensible woman might conclude that is unsafe."

"And yet I encountered you doing exactly the same thing."

I stared right back at her, momentarily forgetting I didn't want anyone paying me too much attention. I didn't know her well enough to tell whether her comment was intended snidely or was a suggestion we both knew more than we said. I might have expected she would explain, or at least offer something else, but she merely continued up the stairs without saying anything else.

I stood there for a few moments, too surprised at her abrupt departure to know whether I should call some farewell after her or just keep going myself. But by the time I turned around, she had already reached the next floor and disappeared from my sight.

As I walked on, I wished Ettu was with me. She would have some comment to make, perhaps something that would even make sense of Amanitore's strange behaviour. The other Ornaments I had met were scrupulously polite, even when making a barbed comment, and I didn't quite know how to react when faced with such rudeness.

At the front doors, Khaemope and Karpusa had been replaced with the night guards, two men whose names I couldn't remember other than that they were impossibly long. I nodded at them as I passed. They returned my nod, but didn't smile or greet me as Khaemope and Karpusa would have.

I didn't let myself think as I chose a path. I wouldn't wonder whether I might run into Khaemmalu. He could be patrolling a different area of the grounds tonight, and even if he saw me, he mightn't reveal himself. Still, I found myself listening for any indication that someone might be nearby.

It was only as I reached the clearing that I realised where my feet had taken me. This was the place where I had first seen the seer. She had been crouched by those flowers over there and seemed to whisper to them. Did they speak to her the way they spoke to me in my dream? Their words had been tantalisingly close when I first woke, then faded away. I remembered standing in front of the narcissus and understanding them, although I couldn't have said whether I heard them with my ears, or if their message somehow just appeared in my mind.

It was too ridiculous, the thoughts of a mad woman. Flowers speaking to me in my mind? If I told anyone about such a thing, they would summon a healer, or a priestess. I finally realised I had ventured away from the torch-lined path. This part of the grounds was dark and shadowy, lit only by the light of the half moon. A chill made its way up my spine. Despite what I believed about where the danger lay, it was unwise to wander around in the dark by myself.

As I turned back, it seemed to me someone hid in the shadows beneath the trees. An extra shape where I was sure no tree had stood previously. A guard probably, although an edge of fear crept over me. It wasn't a lion. It couldn't be a lion.

"Who is there?" I called, and if my voice wobbled just the tiniest bit, I doubted it was noticeable.

The shadow moved, as if someone shifted their weight from foot to foot.

"Show yourself," I said, feeling somewhat cross now. Whoever it was, they were trying to make me afraid. Why else would they stand there and not even respond when I called to them. Well, I would not show my fear. I crossed my arms over my chest and glared at the shadow. "Come on. I don't have all night to stand here."

The shadow crept forward and now I was truly afraid, even though I tried not to show it. Had I made a mistake? We knew without doubt that Pharaoh was responsible for the missing women, but someone must be helping him. Maybe several someones. One of his accomplices could be there in the trees right in front of me.

"If you don't reveal yourself immediately, I will scream," I said. "That will draw the guards' attention and they will come running."

The figure said nothing, only continued to stalk towards me. As she passed through a flicker of moonlight that had somehow made its way through the trees, I got the impression of hunched shoulders. I knew who it was.

"Why didn't you speak?" I asked as she emerged from the shadows.

She didn't look as old in the pale moonlight as in the harshness of the sun. Her shoulders were straighter, her back less rounded. She wore no shawl over her head tonight and the moonlight glistened on the scales on her face. She looked magical rather than old.

"I knew you would search for me," she said.

"You were waiting for me?"

I hadn't come to find her. Or had I? I thought of her before I left my bedchamber, but had made no decision to seek her out. Not consciously anyway.

"You desire information," she said.

"I desire the truth."

Were we even talking about the same thing? But I couldn't reveal what I knew without knowing she knew the same.

"You already have all the information you need," she replied. "But you aren't listening."

"Tell me what I'm not listening to."

She blinked. Even her eyelids were scaled.

"The flowers see all," she said. "They hear everything, you realise. Nobody pays attention to the flowers."

"I don't understand."

"If you listen hard enough, they will tell you what they know."

She retreated back into the shadows beneath the trees. It seemed she had revealed all she intended to.

"Wait," I called after her. "Flowers don't speak."

But she was already gone. I had forgotten how fast she could move, despite her age. But was she really as old as she appeared? Was she even real? No, she was real. Ettu saw her today, and had had seen her that first time too. I hadn't imagined that. I distinctly remembered her commenting on the scales on the woman's face. And Tiye knew her. She told me the woman had a reputation as something of a seer but was unreliable.

I was tempted to follow her, but she could have gone in any direction once she disappeared into the shadows. I hurried back towards the torch-lit path, not wanting to be surprised by anyone else who might be loitering in the dark.

CHAPTER 33

As I made my way back along the path, a bush rustled. That was how Khaemmalu usually let me know he was there, and sure enough, he emerged a few moments later.

"Kassaya." His voice was warm and intimate, and I didn't miss the fact he omitted using my title.

"I didn't expect to see you tonight." I hoped my tone was cool enough to hide how badly I had wanted to see him.

"Why not?" he asked. "I'm here every night."

I stammered, caught off guard.

"I thought you would have shown yourself sooner if you were here," I said. "I walked for some time and never saw you."

"I know."

"You were watching me?"

Shouldn't I have felt his eyes on me? Although I knew I was in no danger from Khaemmalu, it was unsettling to realise I hadn't sensed his presence.

"Of course." He studied me calmly, and although the flickering torchlight revealed his face, I couldn't tell what he was thinking. His next words made it clear he had indeed been watching me. "She is an unusual woman."

"Tiye said she is a seer."

"I have heard that about her."

"Tiye also said she is unreliable."

Khaemmalu tipped his head to the side as he studied me.

"Why, then, did you seek her out?" he asked.

"Do you think she's really a seer?"

He wouldn't miss the fact that I didn't answer his question, but I couldn't tell him the truth. Better not to say anything at all if I couldn't be truthful with him.

Khaemmalu shrugged. "I have no reason not to believe it. I have never spoken to her myself, though. Never even heard her speak before tonight. She always gives me a wide berth, even when she shouldn't know I'm there."

He tipped his head slightly to the side, gesturing towards the bushes.

"Come with me," he said.

I followed him into the shadows. As the darkness enveloped us, his fingers found mine, leading me on.

I held his hand, marvelling at the warmth of his skin and the thrill it sent through me. Surely we were safe here beneath the cover of the trees and the darkness. He led me to a spot where no shrubbery grew beneath the spreading branches of an acacia tree. Khaemmalu dropped my hand as he leaned against the trunk.

He suddenly felt so far away. The hand he had held tingled and itched to reach for him. I clutched my skirt, grasping the linen tightly enough to wrinkle the fabric, but it stopped me from reaching for his hand.

"Why were you looking for the seer, Kassaya?" Khaemmalu's voice was low.

"She has been trying to tell me something."

"What?" he asked. Then when I hesitated, "have I not proved I can keep your secrets?"

"She thinks I should leave."

The words slid out of my mouth without any thought. I hadn't meant to tell him, but something about Khaemmalu made me want to do anything he said. Everything he said. The thought caught me off guard and I took a step back, away from him. As if it was his nearness that made me say what I hadn't intended to.

Khaemmalu peeled himself off the trunk and took a single step towards me, closing the gap I had just opened.

"Why does she think you should leave?" he asked.

"She said I shouldn't get involved in something that is coming."

He studied me, his head tipped to the side. If he knew what the seer meant, he gave no sign of it.

"Do you know what she refers to?" he asked.

"No."

It wasn't a lie. I suspected some plot or other was being developed. The Ornaments' business Tiye didn't want to share with me, at least. But I had no solid information. Or maybe the seer meant my own plan for revenge? I had only discussed that with Ahmose, but if the scaled woman was truly a seer, that didn't mean she didn't know.

"Kassaya." Khaemmalu took another half step forward and now he was so close, I could feel his breath on my face. "Perhaps you should take her advice."

"You think I should leave?" I searched his face for answers, but could see little except shadowy pools where his eyes were.

"This place," he said. "It is not somewhere I would want

anyone I cared about to be. Terrible things happen here and there are those who are working to put a stop to them."

My breath hitched. Was he hinting he cared about me? I almost missed the significance of his words.

"Like the women who disappear?" I asked. "Or are there other things I don't know about yet?"

He stepped back, not far, but enough that the moment no longer felt quite so intimate.

"You should leave if you can." His voice was more normal now. Less husky. "Would your father send for you if he knew about your sister?"

"I don't know. There is still the alliance to consider."

I didn't like to think Father might leave me here, even once he knew Ishtar was dead, but it was possible. Perhaps even probable. He wouldn't risk the alliance. Wouldn't risk bringing war to Babylon's shores for the sake of a daughter who had already been traded. I was Pharaoh's property now and no longer my father's.

"I would help you," he said. "If you wanted to leave."

"I have been told we are not allowed to leave. That once we are here, we stay, at least until we are too old to bear children."

My son. He still didn't know, but this wasn't the moment to tell him.

"Before you came here, I'd never once broken a rule," he said. "Never even considered it. I know the penalties and I would rather keep my life, and my job, than risk them both. But you..." His voice trailed away and he studied me, his gaze molten now. The heat of his stare seeped through my skin and into my veins. "You make me forget to be sensible."

My mouth went dry and I couldn't have spoken, even if I thought of something to say.

"You feel it too." He moved forward, once again closing the gap between us. His fingers grazed mine, although he stopped short of taking hold of my hand. "There is something between us and I wish we had met under other circumstances."

"The penalty for an affair is death." My voice was no more than a whisper and even as close as he was, I wasn't sure he would hear me. "Would you really risk that?"

"For you? Yes. But you didn't answer my question."

I couldn't remember what he had asked.

"Do you feel it?" He edged closer and now we stood chest-to-chest, not quite touching. The heat from his body drifted towards me.

When I didn't reply, he raised his hand and trailed one finger ever so gently along my jaw.

"Tell me, Kassaya," he breathed.

"I do," I whispered.

It was all I could say, but it was enough.

Khaemmalu closed the gap between us and his mouth touched mine. His finger left my jaw and he set his hand on my cheek, holding me firmly to his mouth. My mind went blank, my legs were weak, and it was all I could do to remain on my feet.

It was only as his lips left mine, that I realised my eyes were closed. When I opened them, he was looking at me with such tenderness that I almost wept. He dropped his hand from my cheek, letting it fall to my shoulder, then slide down my arm until he captured my hand.

"The first time I saw you," he said. "I knew I wanted to know you."

"I was so embarrassed." My cheeks heated as I remembered our first meeting. He found us on the path between the gates and the Palace shortly after we arrived, still confused about why we hadn't been given admittance to Pharaoh's palace. "I was worried you thought I was flirting with you."

He laughed a little.

"I thought you were friendly," he said. "But this place changes people and I knew you might be different by the time I saw you next."

"And was I?"

"No. Not then. You are changed now, though. Harder, I think. Less innocent."

His words brought me back to my senses. What was I doing? I risked both our lives if we were caught like this. I stepped back, releasing his hands, even though it sorrowed me to do so.

"Kassaya?" He sounded confused.

"I'm sorry," I said. "The risk…"

"Of course." His face changed, becoming once again the blank mask I was used to seeing on Pharaoh's guards. "Allow me to escort you back to the path. It would seem you lost your way in the dark."

CHAPTER 34

"How was your walk?" Sehener asked as she let me back into my chambers.

To both her surprise and mine, I burst into tears.

"My lady?"

I heard the soft thunk of the bar dropping into place, then she took me by the arm.

"Come," she said. "Sit down. I will pour you some wine. Should I wake Ahmose? She could prepare a brew to calm you."

I wiped my tears on my sleeve and sniffled.

"No, I am well enough," I said. "I think I will just go to bed."

I left the sitting chamber before Sehener could press me any further. Back in my bed, I must have fallen asleep almost immediately, although I expected to do no more than toss and turn. After all, how would I sleep after Khaemmalu had kissed me? How could anyone who knew the secrets the Palace kept ever sleep again?

But I woke as the bird outside my window began its

dawn song. I lay there for a while, trying to grasp the lingering threads of my dream. Something about Khaemmalu and lions and the seer, but it was all jumbled together and I couldn't make any sense of it. The only thing I knew with certainty was that Khaemmalu had held my hand. He had kissed me.

I felt too tired to bother getting up, but although I longed to go back to sleep, I couldn't get comfortable again. The air in my bedchamber was already too warm and my lower back ached. My stomach felt odd too. Perhaps my unease had disturbed the babe. I gave up and got out of bed.

In the sitting chamber, Ettu and Sehener were already up. They sat in facing chairs as they chatted, their hands already busy with needlework. They stopped when they saw me and the looks on their faces said quite clearly they had been talking about me. Discussing last night's tears no doubt. Before anyone could speak, a knock came and Ettu went to let Merytre in. She carried a bunch of narcissus and offered us a sunny smile.

"I saw these on my way through the grounds and thought you might like some in here," she said to me, tilting the flowers in my direction. "They are so cheery, are they not? You seemed to like the ones Sehener brought the other week."

"Indeed." I could hardly tell her my interest in the narcissus was only because I kept dreaming they talked to me.

Merytre busied herself with finding a vase for the flowers. Tall emerged from his bedchamber, and soon enough the kitchen servants brought our breakfast. Then my maids arrived. As they prepared me for the day, I occupied myself with thoughts of Khaemmalu and our kiss.

"My lady, are you well?" Nebetah asked as she arranged my wig. "Your cheeks are rather flushed."

Of course, my traitorous cheeks heated even more at her question.

"Quite fine."

I tried to push away my thoughts, but they kept returning. The look on Khaemmalu's face as he drew nearer to me. The way his fingers grazed mine. The softness of his lips. He made me feel… something. Something I had no words to describe and which was entirely unexpected. After all, I was hardly an innocent anymore. I had lain with a man and I carried his child in my belly. But Pharaoh didn't make me feel the way Khaemmalu did. I supposed lying with Khaemmalu might be very different to being with Pharaoh.

"Your skin is hot," Tuya said, pressing her palm to my arm as she pushed a silver armband into place. "Perhaps you are sickening."

"Maybe you should return to bed," Ipu suggested. "I could go to the kitchens and fetch you some soup."

"Tell them to be sure it has lots of onions in it," Nebetah advised her. "When my little sister was unwell, the healer told us to feed her onions."

"We could summon a priestess to pray over you," Mutnofret said.

"And a healer," Khensa added with a vigorous nod that sent her braids swinging. "When my mother fell ill last *akhet*, a healer came and performed incantations. We were sure she would go to the West, but she improved almost immediately after the healer's visit."

"Was it a full recovery?" Mutnofret asked.

"Oh, yes," Khensa said. "And it was all thanks to the healer and her incantations."

"I don't need a healer," I said. "Or soup, or onions, or a priestess. I am perfectly well."

"It is rather hot today," Ettu said. "Perhaps your bathing water was too warm and left you overheated."

"Yes, that's probably it." I shot her a grateful look, but Ettu busied herself rearranging the cosmetics jars and seemed not to notice.

Abar, as usual, stood off to the side and made no effort to participate in the conversation. When my maids left, I was surprised to see her still there. Normally, she would be the first out the door. Sehener returned a wig to its shelf and Ettu was still fussing with the cosmetics. Abar stayed where she was, one hip jutting out to the side.

"Something you want to say?" I asked.

She wasn't looking at me, but I couldn't think of any other reason she would still be here.

"I sent a message to my sister," she said.

"Is she well?"

Abar shrugged.

"She has not replied," she mumbled.

"Maybe she is busy with her duties," I said. "I'm sure she will reply when she can."

Abar glared at me and I was almost relieved to see her usual fire return. I didn't know how to respond to this version of her which seemed sad rather than angry.

"Maybe you didn't tell me the truth," she said.

"Excuse me?"

"I don't believe my sister is really at Pharaoh's palace. She would have replied immediately. She would not leave me waiting."

"Perhaps she hasn't yet received your message," I said. "Did you send it through the Palace scribe?"

"Of course not." She gave me a scathing look. "He does not send messages for the likes of me, and he would not know our language anyway. I sent it with a runner boy who was delivering other messages there."

Ettu had finally finished rearranging the cosmetics jars and came to put her hand on Abar's shoulder.

"Maybe the boy didn't deliver it," she said gently. "Or maybe he gave it to the wrong woman or there was some other confusion."

"I assure you," Abar said stiffly, "there was no confusion. And he was adequately paid for his services. If I find out he didn't deliver the message to my sister after that, he will feel my wrath."

I wondered exactly how she had paid the runner boy, but at seeing the look on Ettu's face, decided not to ask.

"Then you must assume she has been unable to reply for some reason," Ettu said. "She is too busy, or there was no runner available, or something else we have not thought of."

"I think she lied." Abar shot me a venomous look. "My sister is not really in Pharaoh's palace."

"That is enough." Ettu's voice was sharp now. "We are finished here and you may go."

Abar stomped across the chamber. She paused in the doorway and looked back at me.

"You had best pray to your Babylonian gods," she said. "If you lied to me, you will be sorry."

She was gone before either Ettu or I could say anything else.

"Well," Ettu said eventually. "It would seem she thinks you have the power to control what happens in Pharaoh's palace."

I was still trying to gather my thoughts, stunned at Abar's threat.

"I will arrange for her to be reassigned, of course," Ettu

said. "You will not want her to serve you any longer after that."

I nodded, but as we made our way out to the sitting chamber, I reconsidered.

"Don't," I said to Ettu.

"Don't?" she asked.

"Don't have Abar reassigned."

"But…" Ettu's voice trailed off as she examined me with a dubious look. "I know well enough that if you have decided, there will be no convincing you otherwise. But I urge you to reconsider. She made a direct threat to you. She could be dangerous."

"She is hardly more than a girl. What danger could she be to me? I am never even alone with her."

"You don't need to be alone with her for her to cause trouble. Have you forgotten what Nammu did?"

"Of course not."

But Nammu had reason to hate me, or at least she thought she did. She claimed Ishtar said I had specifically asked for her to be sent with me to Egypt. It wasn't true, of course, and I bitterly regretted I never found the right time to ask Ishtar whether she really said that. I would never know now. Was Abar's reason any less than Nammu's? If Abar thought I had lied and deliberately withheld her sister's location, might she do something to act on her threat?

"Just don't trust her," Ettu advised. "At least think about having her reassigned, but if you decide not to, don't trust her. I think that girl will turn out to be trouble."

I only nodded, my thoughts too tangled to venture a reply.

It wasn't until later that afternoon that Ettu mentioned last night's walk. By then, I had decided Sehener mustn't have told her after all, but it seemed Ettu was merely waiting until we were alone in the sitting chamber.

"Sehener said you went for a walk last night. Alone." Her voice was cool, the disapproving tone she used when she was unhappy with me.

"I needed some air." I had never cared for needlework, but in this moment I regretted not having something I could focus on without looking like I was trying to avoid her eyes.

"Hmm."

Ettu said nothing else. I was relieved, if also surprised, that she would let me off so lightly. But only moments passed before she spoke again.

"Sehener also said you returned in tears."

"It was nothing," I said.

She frowned and didn't look convinced.

"I was feeling emotional," I added. "It must be the babe. Ahmose said I might not feel like myself."

"Did something happen while you were walking?" Ettu asked.

"Of course not."

"You know it's not safe to be out alone," she said. "If something happened, you need to tell us, so we can take extra precautions in future."

"Nothing happened."

She looked steadily at me and said nothing. I crumbled under her stare.

"I saw Khaemmalu," I admitted.

"And he made you cry?" Ettu hesitated, as if considering her words. "I thought I sensed an attraction between the two of you. Did you argue?"

"No."

She raised her eyebrows and waited. I cast my gaze around

the sitting chamber, searching for a way to avoid saying anything else. It was on the tip of my tongue, but what was the point? There could never be anything between Khaemmalu and me. The risk was too great, for both of us.

"If you didn't argue, then something else happened," Ettu said. "You wouldn't return in tears just because you spoke with him. Unless he had new information about Lady Ishtar?"

"No," I said quietly. "He didn't."

For a few hours, I had forgotten all about Ishtar. How could I have forgotten, however briefly?

"Then something happened," she said.

Ettu was still studying me. The look on her face said quite clearly she knew I was lying. If I didn't tell her, she would think I didn't trust her. But if I did, she would know how foolish I had been. Which would be worse?

"Khaemmalu touched me," I said, my voice low. It still felt too new, too precious to tell anyone. I was only telling Ettu so she would stop pestering me.

"Where?" she asked.

"In the grounds."

Ettu huffed. "Where on your body did he touch you?"

"My arm," I admitted. "My hand."

I wouldn't tell her he had kissed me. That I would keep to myself.

"I'm sure you are well aware of the consequences if the administrators were to find out," she said. "As is he."

"Yes," I said. "It won't happen again, you can be sure of that."

Tall's return interrupted our conversation. He gave us a broad smile and went to stand in his usual place beside the window.

"You look rather cheery today," Ettu said.

Tall darted a glance over his shoulder, as if checking it was he she spoke to. Ettu gave him exactly the same look she had given me. I studied Tall more carefully. What had she noticed that I hadn't? He did look happy, and had been for the last few days. He seemed to have shaken off the moroseness he fell into after he and Half fled Pharaoh's palace. He said as little as ever, but I hadn't noticed him flapping his hands or pacing the chamber for several days now.

"Happy!" Tall said, clearly realising Ettu wouldn't stop until he gave her something.

"Yes, I noticed that," she said archly. "I also noticed Sehener seems particularly happy too."

I blinked in surprise. Had something developed between Tall and Sehener? I had noticed they often sat together, and she seemed to intuitively understand him in a way nobody else did. Tall had even managed to start speaking a few words of Egyptian since he had met her. But I had thought it no more than a friendship. A companionship as a result of their proximity. Tall flapped his hands and didn't reply. To my surprise, Ettu laughed.

"It's all right," she said to him. "You don't need to tell me. I'm merely pleased to see you both happy."

"You didn't say that to me," I muttered.

She shot me a loaded look.

"The consequences are different for you," she said. "As you are well aware."

I swallowed my reply. Whatever I said now would probably be the wrong thing. Thankfully, Sehener returned at that moment and Ettu surely no longer expected my reply.

"Are you feeling better today, my lady?" Sehener asked.

"I am well enough," I said. "I find myself feeling very

emotional these days. The slightest thing seems to provoke me to tears."

"It is probably the babe," Ahmose said as she came in. "Some women feel very odd while they are pregnant. Happy one moment, sad the next. The babe must have some effect on your blood to cause such a thing."

She had been rising later recently, often not emerging from her bed until well after my maids arrived. Her long braids were in disarray and she squinted at me, as if she wasn't quite sure she was awake yet.

I made a noncommittal noise and hoped that would be the end of the conversation. For now, at least. It was too much to expect they would forget.

CHAPTER 35

As I left Tiye's chambers, Abar was on my mind. Her certainty that her sister would have replied to her message had she received it bothered me. Tiye had already asked Panouk about Atahar and I couldn't ask her to check again. I'd have to ask him myself.

"I want to speak with Panouk," I said to Ettu.

"Now?"

"Yes. Where would I find him?"

"He has an office on the ground floor," she said. "I think I know where it is."

To my surprise, she didn't ask why I wanted to see him, only led me downstairs where she found his office on the second try. Panouk sat in a comfortable chair, his feet propped up on a stool as he studied a scroll.

"Lady Kassaya," he said, setting the scroll aside as he spotted us in the doorway. "Is there a problem?"

"I believe Tiye asked you about a particular servant," I said. "One from Nubia."

"Yes, yes," he said quickly. "As I told her, our records indicate the girl was assigned to Pharaoh's palace. Laundry duties."

"Is there a way to confirm whether she still works there?" I asked.

He gave me a quizzical look.

"I suppose I could send a message," he conceded. "May I ask why it concerns you?"

"Her sister is one of my lady's maids."

"I see." He studied me as if waiting for more.

"She asked me to check on her sister."

"You are exceedingly generous to help her," he said.

His overt obsequiousness grated on my nerves.

"She is concerned for her sister," I said, my tone shorter now. "She has sent a message, but received no reply."

"I will arrange for a messenger," Panouk said. "And I will personally inform you of what he learns."

As we made our way back to my chambers, I noticed Ettu frowning.

"What is it?" I asked. "Do you think he will not do it?"

"No, I'm sure he will," she said. "He can hardly do anything else now he has told you he will."

"Then why do you frown?"

She sighed and shook her head.

"Something bothers me," she said. "I can't quite figure out what."

"About Abar?"

"Her sister."

We reached my chambers and she knocked on the door.

"It's probably nothing," she said.

Sehener let us in and hurried off to unlock Tall's door. The other women were in their favourite chairs, Merytre with some stitching on her lap.

"Started something new?" Ettu asked, stopping beside Merytre to inspect her stitching.

Merytre smoothed the linen so she could see it.

"It's for my lady's bedchamber," she said. "Since she likes those flowers so much."

"Very pretty," Ettu said. "You have a delicate hand with the petals."

Merytre held up the linen to show me. A yellow narcissus gleamed against the white fabric, its petals spread open like a mouth. As if it was about to speak. The sight chilled me. Between the narcissus and the lions, it felt increasingly like someone was sending me a message I couldn't interpret. Surely only the gods could do such a thing, though.

"Lovely," I said.

"I thought it would look nice beside your window," Merytre said. "Of course, you can put it anywhere you want to, and maybe you don't even want it in your bedchamber at all."

"I'm sure it will be beautiful."

I could hardly tell her a narcissus was the last thing I wanted in my bedchamber.

The following day, Panouk rapped on the door. Merytre waited until Tall was safely locked away before she let him in.

"Lady Kassaya." Panouk gave me a brief bow. I eyed him from my couch, noting the way he shuffled his feet. I had never seen him look discomfited before.

"Do you have news for me?" I asked.

"Yes." He paused to clear his throat. "As a matter of fact, I do."

I waited, but he said nothing further.

"Well?" I prompted.

"Well," he said. "As it happens, ah, you see."

I narrowed my eyes at him and hoped it made my gaze look as frosty as my mother's. It must have worked because he wiped his brow and stood a little straighter.

"Lady Kassaya, I have investigated the matter you raised with me yesterday and I am afraid the girl is, uh…"

I waited.

"The thing is, she appears to be gone," he said finally.

As he said it, a deep sense of inevitability filled me and I found I wasn't surprised. Until this moment, I had honestly believed it was all a misunderstanding. A miscommunication perhaps. That Atahar was still there in Pharaoh's palace and there was a perfectly good reason she never replied to Abar's message. But now it had been said, it felt like the very thing I had expected him to say all along.

"Where is she then?" I asked.

Panouk cleared his throat and wiped his forehead again.

"The messenger was unable to find anyone who knew," he said. "She hasn't been seen for some time. Weeks, at least. Maybe as long as a couple of months."

And the pieces finally fell into place. I had known the answer all along. I had seen her, after all. Her dark-skinned limbs neatly laid out on the workbench. Her face turned towards the doorway as if she waited for someone to arrive. The way she never moved as the dagger parted her belly.

The unknown woman in the House of Life was Abar's sister, Atahar.

CHAPTER 36

*P*anouk left as quickly as he could after delivering his news. Ettu slipped away to unlock Tall's door, and for a few moments, there was silence in the sitting chamber.

"Well," Ettu said when she returned with Tall. "I suspect we are all thinking the same thing."

"It was her," Merytre said sadly. "The woman we saw."

"I think so too," Ettu said.

I swallowed and could only nod. Tall said nothing, but then he hadn't ever seen Abar since he was always locked away when my maids were here. He wouldn't know that her skin was the exact same shade as that of the woman in the House of Life. He wouldn't realise Abar's long fingers were just like her sister's. How many times had I seen her hands as she passed Ettu my jewels, and yet I had never really noticed them. Had I looked harder, I might have realised sooner.

But then, Abar was hardly the only woman in this place with skin so black. There was Amanitore, for one, and many others I saw every day. So many that it never occurred to me the woman we saw might be Abar's sister. Yet I had known Abar had a sister and that she didn't know where the girl was. If only I had thought to ask after her sister's location sooner, we might have realised.

"I will have to tell her," I said.

Silence greeted my words. I waited, but still nobody said anything.

"What?" I asked. "Surely you don't disagree. I have to tell her."

"Do you think that is wise?" Ettu spoke slowly, as if choosing her words with extreme care.

"I told her I would find out where her sister was."

"You saw the way she reacted yesterday," Ettu said. "When she thought you had lied to her. We don't know with certainty the woman we saw was Atahar."

"Many captives were brought from Nubia at the same time as Abar and Atahar," Merytre added.

"The woman you saw might not even have been one of the palace staff," Sehener said. So, someone had obviously told her of our illicit expedition to the House of Life. Ettu most probably. "She might be someone who lives in Thebes, or was merely passing through at the time she went to the West."

"What if you tell Abar and later learn you were wrong?" Ettu asked. "She will have grieved her sister for nothing. However upset she might be to learn her sister has died, it will be nothing compared to finding out it wasn't true."

Tall said nothing, not that I would expect him to. I looked to Ahmose, since she was the only other who hadn't commented yet. She gave me her usual steady look.

"You will do as you choose, of course," she said. "But you have received some wise advice here today. My only suggestion is that you should think hard on their words."

"If you must tell her," Ettu said. "At least keep it to what Panouk told you. Don't tell her we think we saw her in the House of Life."

She was right, of course. No matter how much I wanted to tell Abar everything I knew about her sister, I couldn't reveal we had snuck out. News of something like that would spread far too quickly if Abar was inclined to tell anyone, and it would not be long before the administrators heard of it. Even if there was no proof, they would surely come to question me. And how long would it be before they decided to search my chambers for evidence of my having left the Palace grounds? No, it was far too dangerous to tell Abar that much.

"Do!" Tall said at last.

I hadn't expected him to offer any comment by this point. Was he saying he thought I should tell Abar? If so, he would be the only one who agreed with me. As was often the case these days, it was Sehener who understood him first.

"You worry what Abar might do when she finds out?" she asked him.

Tall flapped his hands and she reached out to take one. I expected him to pull away from her, perhaps tumble off the couch in his hurry to escape as he had when I touched him like that, but although he startled, he allowed her to hold his hand. He frowned and I could see how much effort he put into trying to make the right words come from his mouth.

"Angry!" he said.

"Yes, she might be," Sehener said.

"Door!"

Sehener looked to me, obviously expecting I understood him.

"You suggest we don't lock you in when I tell Abar?" I asked, unsure whether that was what he really meant.

Tall nodded, pulling his fingers from Sehener's grip to flap his hands again.

"It's too dangerous," I said. "What if someone found you?"

"There would be no reason for anyone to try the door to his bedchamber," Ettu said. "Your lady's maids are accustomed to it being locked, and so long as the door is closed, there is no way to tell it isn't by merely looking at it."

"You sound like you agree with him," I said.

Ettu shrugged. "I think it too risky, but if Abar reacts violently, we might need Tall."

"And then she will have seen him," I pointed out. "What then? Do I lock her in a bedchamber as well? We can hardly let her go once she knows Tall is here."

"I don't know." Ettu sounded a little irritable now. "I only think we need to consider all possibilities and be as prepared as we can. We have no way of knowing how Abar will react and it seems you insist on telling her."

"Folk react to distressing news in all sorts of ways," Ahmose said. "Perhaps she will surprise us."

As my maids flocked around me the following morning and I waited for the moment when I would deliver the terrible news to Abar, my heart raced. My hands shook, and I couldn't quite catch my breath, even though I did nothing more than sit on a stool while Nebetah applied my makeup and the others bickered about which sandals would look best with the gown they had chosen. At last, they pronounced me ready. As usual, Abar was the first to the door.

"Abar," I called. "Please wait."

I didn't miss the way her shoulders stiffened. She stood aside while the others filed out. Abar's face was sullen and her gaze was fixed on the floor.

"Come here," I said, trying to make my voice gentle.

She came slowly. Unwillingly. I wondered if she sensed I had bad news to share or if she expected to be rebuked for something. Certainly the look on her face suggested she thought she was about to be punished, perhaps for threatening me the other day.

"Abar, I have news of your sister," I said.

Her gaze flew up to meet mine and she froze at whatever she saw there.

"It isn't good, I'm afraid," I said.

"Tell me." Her voice was soft, the usual belligerence gone.

"She was indeed assigned to the laundry in Pharaoh's palace as I was told previously. But when I asked for confirmation she was still there, I was advised..." My courage faltered and my voice trailed away.

"Hurry up," she said brusquely.

"She disappeared some weeks ago," I said. "I'm very sorry to tell you, but it is believed she met with some accident that caused her death."

None of us had speculated on how Atahar met her end, although surely they all wondered the same thing as I did: was Pharaoh responsible? There was no way to know whether a new laundry servant might have caught his eye, and I wanted to spare Abar the heartache of this, at least.

I might have expected her to burst into tears at such news, but the girl was stronger than that. She only gave me a steely look and waited.

"That is all I can tell you," I said. "I am so sorry."

"You *think* she had an accident?" Abar's voice was cool. "You *think* my sister is dead?"

"Well, yes," I floundered.

"You think?" she yelled. "You think? You did not even bother to confirm, you only think?"

"That is what I was advised." Had I made a mistake in insisting Tall be locked in his bedchamber as usual? Would she attack me? "There can be no certainty without—"

I stopped abruptly as I realised what I had been about to say. No certainty without a body.

"I understand how difficult it is to hear such news," I said. "My sister—"

"Do not presume you know anything about me." Abar's voice was stiff now. "You know nothing about what it is like to be taken from your home to be a slave in a foreign land."

I knew a little more than she realised, but I kept my mouth shut. It would only incense her further if I tried to tell her that I, too, had been sent from my home without my agreement. My situation here was vastly different from hers. I lived in luxury with servants to do anything I wanted. Abar did not. Although I understood something of her situation, I could never know exactly what she had experienced.

"You did this to punish me," Abar spat. "Because I am not a meek, subservient slave like your maids here. You had her killed the way you did your own sister."

I only blinked at her, too shocked to reply.

"Abar, enough," Ettu snapped.

If Abar even heard her, she gave no sign of it.

"If she is dead, it is your fault," she said. "If you had found her quicker, I could have gone to her. We could have left this wretched place. She would not be dead if you had done what you said you would."

She stormed away, leaving me open-mouthed in her wake.

"Well," Ettu said. "I can't say I have changed my opinion that you should have her reassigned."

"She thinks it is my fault." There was no need to say it. They could hardly have avoided hearing.

"She is distraught," Merytre said. "She doesn't really believe that."

"She lashed out at you because she knows you will forgive her," Sehener added. "She surely blames you no more than any of us do."

But Abar said she did blame me, and she wasn't the first to accuse me to my face of being responsible for Ishtar's death. Perhaps I should have spread my own gossip after all. No, that was not the kind of person I was. I would model myself on Ettu. If it was her accused of such an awful thing, she would hold her head high and give no sign it bothered her. That was what I would do.

"I know you have reason to be sympathetic towards her situation," Ettu said. "But this only makes it more urgent that you request she be reassigned."

"Or dismissed even," Merytre said. "She did threaten you, after all."

We went out to the sitting chamber. Sehener unlocked Tall's door on the way and he followed us down the hallway. There was no need to explain to him what had happened. He could hardly have avoided hearing. I settled myself on the couch and smoothed out my skirt before the fine linen could wrinkle.

"It was a terrible shock for her." I knew all too well what it was like to receive such news. "She needs our support right now, not our condemnation."

"She could cause trouble for you," Merytre said.

"I agree," Sehener added quickly. "I have never heard someone speak with such venom. I know her situation is very difficult, and I have tried to be sympathetic to that, but I agree my lady ought to have her reassigned."

"What trouble could she cause?" I asked. "If she went to

Panouk and accused me of being responsible for her sister's death, I doubt he would take her seriously. Especially after I was the one who asked him to confirm her safety."

"What if she suspects something of the secrets we keep here?" Merytre asked. "She may have seen or heard something. It might be nothing much. An insignificant detail. But enough for her to tell the administrators something is being concealed here."

"And if they came to search your chambers, it would not take long to realise there is a door that never had a lock on it before," Ettu said. "They would surely want to see what is behind it."

"I knew there was some secret," Sehener added. "Although I'm not sure I could say exactly how, and of course, I had no idea what it was."

Before I could respond, a knock came at the door. We froze. My heart pounded an alarm. Had Abar already gone to the administrators? Was that Panouk come to see whether there was any truth to her tale that something illicit had occurred within my chambers? The knock sounded again and at last it was Ettu who got to her feet. Tall slipped away and Sehener followed to lock him in again.

"Who is it?" Ettu asked at the door. She made no move to unbar it as she waited for Sehener's return.

"Message for the Lady Kassaya," came a young male voice. "From Pharaoh himself."

Sehener came back and nodded at Ettu to indicate Tall was safely locked away. Ettu raised the bar and opened the door. A runner of perhaps eleven years waited there. He gave her a perfunctory bow, then cleared his throat.

"Pharaoh Ramses, Mighty Bull, Strong and Valiant like Montu, Rich in Years Like Ptah, the King of Upper and Lower

Egypt requests the presence of the Lady Kassaya from Babylon for a game of *senet* tomorrow afternoon," he said. "She is to attend him at his palace."

"My lady would be pleased to accept," Ettu said.

The runner bowed again and hurried away. Ettu closed the door and leaned against it, her hand over her heart.

"I honestly thought it would be Panouk," she said with a small laugh. "Silly really. Even if Abar had gone straight to him, he surely wouldn't be here so soon. She could hardly have found him in the time since she left and also convinced him to search your chambers already."

"I thought it too," I said.

If any of them wondered whether I would be safe in Pharaoh's palace, they didn't say it.

CHAPTER 37

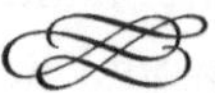

As I sat in Tiye's chambers a short while later, I sensed she had something on her mind. Perhaps she too was thinking about our last conversation. Although I longed to ask what else she knew about Pharaoh's crimes and about those women who had left the Palace after their childbearing years were over, I held my tongue. She would tell me in her own time if I was patient.

Tiye spoke of nothing of any consequence. She offered pleasantries on the weather, which was still hot with no sign of the promised cooler days to come, and shared some choice gossip, although nothing I had come hoping to hear. She would have undoubtedly heard about Panouk's message to confirm Abar's sister was still in Pharaoh's palace, but she didn't mention it. If Panouk had learned something else which he had decided not to share with me, Tiye would be the one to know. I was fairly sure she would tell me.

"Pharaoh intends to play *senet* tomorrow," Tiye said eventually, seemingly having run out of other news. She gave me a cool look. "Although I suspect you already know."

"He has invited me to play with him." If I wasn't watching so carefully, I might have missed the way she sat up a little straighter.

"Do you play well?" she asked. "You certainly didn't the time we played."

I laughed. "Hardly. That was the only time I've played. I think I understand the rules, but I'm afraid I am a poor player."

"Good," she said as she leaned back against the couch.

"Why?"

"Because there's one thing you must always keep in mind if Pharaoh invites you to play *senet*. He likes to win."

I shrugged. It was no more than she had said previously.

"Doesn't everyone?" I asked.

Tiye looked me right in the eyes and the look on her face chilled me.

"You misunderstand me, Kassaya, so let me say this plainly. If you play against Pharaoh, let him win. Every time."

"Why? He's hardly going to…"

Her expression never changed and my voice trailed away.

"You don't mean… He would hardly…" I couldn't say it. Wasn't even quite sure what I was trying to say.

"Don't underestimate him, Kassaya," Tiye said. "He likes to win and he likes you to fear him. That combination can be deadly."

Since she seemed amenable to sharing secrets, maybe this would be a good moment to push her. I took a breath to steady myself.

"What exactly was the 'business' you didn't want to discuss in front of me?" I asked.

"At Ineni's gathering?" Her gaze flicked up to meet mine.

"Yes." I studied her face, wondering whether this would be

the point where she would stop talking. When she hesitated, I let out an exasperated sigh. "You still don't trust me? Even after I have told you how much I already know?"

"It's dangerous," she said. "You can't even begin to comprehend how dangerous. Are you sure you want to know?"

"Can it be any worse than what I already know?"

She only eyed me.

"I know more than I have said," I told her. "Why don't we share our information?"

"Go on, then." She lifted her chin in my direction, an indication for me to speak. "Tell me what you think you know."

I prayed to Marduk I wasn't making a terrible mistake.

"Pharaoh's captain and his second dispose of the bodies once Pharaoh has finished with them," I said.

I stared her right in the eyes, daring her to contradict me. To my surprise, she flinched and looked away, as if to compose herself.

"I didn't think you knew any more than I told you," she said at last. "Although that was probably enough for you to draw some conclusions of your own."

"It took me longer than it should have to figure out."

"I'm truly sorry about your sister," she said. "When she caught his eye so quickly, I feared for her. And for you," she added. "I worried you might act incautiously if you suspected the truth."

"You thought I would confront Pharaoh?" I asked.

"Perhaps."

Tiye shrugged and somehow the movement was as elegant as ever, despite the awfulness of our conversation. She hesitated and I honestly thought she didn't intend to tell me about their business.

"We have a plan," she said at last. "Ineni, Neferu, Gilukhipa,

Henutmire, and I. We intend to reveal Pharaoh's crimes and deliver justice for what he has done."

So I wasn't the only person who thought we could hold him accountable if we joined together. I had thought their business had something to do with the missing women, but hadn't guessed they might want the same as I did.

"I have been told they aren't crimes," I said. "That Pharaoh is above the law."

Tiye shrugged. "That may be, but what he does is despicable no matter what you call it."

I'd never heard her criticise him before. Had thought her entire focus was on maintaining her position as Favourite and Top Ornament. But maybe she was only using her position to fulfil her plan.

"So what do you intend to do about it?" I asked.

"He must be removed from the throne," she said. "He does not deserve such a position. We will replace him with my son, Pentaweret."

For a few moments, I could only blink at her.

"You plan to put your son on the throne?" I asked.

She gave me a defiant look. "He is a far better option than Pharaoh's chosen heir. That Ramses is a spoiled wretch. Pentaweret will be a better ruler than either Pharaoh or his heir. We are doing this for the sake of the whole country, not just the women he has killed."

"It's a bold plan." No, it was more than bold. It was audacious. Dangerous. Perhaps even arrogant.

"You could join us," she said. "Work with us to make this happen. I know you well enough by now to know you don't intend to let your sister's death pass without justice. We can help you make that happen."

I dropped my gaze to my hands, not wanting her to see

how close to the truth she had come. I hadn't dare let myself think about what might happen if my plan came to fruition. What exactly I would do once I had enough power to make Pharaoh fear me. I supposed it might mean he was no longer on the throne, but I hadn't considered who would replace him. After all, he already had an heir, and it wasn't my son. It wasn't Tiye's son either. Maybe her goal and mine were much the same. Maybe they weren't.

"I cannot," I said. "There is too much danger in what you propose."

"The world will not change unless there are those of us who are willing to face danger," she said.

I changed the topic, asking instead about Weren, the butler who was still searching for evidence of magic use, although, according to Tiye, he had still found nothing.

I left soon after. Tiye's confession had unnerved me. I, too, had planned to expose Pharaoh, but I only now realised how undeveloped my plan was. It was a dangerous game the other women played. Were they going too far?

As Ettu and I returned to my chambers, I debated whether to share what Tiye had said. Ettu, as observant as ever, shot me a few sideways glances. She obviously guessed something bothered me, but to my surprise, she didn't ask.

I passed the rest of the day feeling like I was far too tightly wound, hardly daring to speak in case what I had learned spilled out of me. I couldn't tell anyone of Tiye's plan to expose Pharaoh's crimes and to put her own son on the throne. I knew too many secrets, and not all of them were my own. How would I ever be able to speak again without risk of some secret or other bursting out of me?

I was still keeping the news of Ishtar's death a secret from my father. I hadn't yet written to him. Had told myself I would wait until we were certain of her fate. Until someone had seen her body. But there was no doubt, was there? If she was alive, we would have learned something about it by now. Tears welled and I blinked hard before they could fall. I had admitted she was dead, but the grief was still raw. Would the day ever come when I could think of her with dry eyes and without this pain in my chest?

"My lady?"

Sehener's soft query broke through into my thoughts. We were gathered in the sitting chamber as usual, all of us except Ahmose who had left shortly after I returned, mumbling about needing to see someone. Her contact, I hoped. The one who was bribing the librarian for me.

"My lady, are you well?" Sehener asked.

"Yes, yes, perfectly." I ducked my head, trying to hide that I brushed away a few stray tears.

"Did Lady Tiye say something to bother you?" Ettu asked.

I had thought her too busy with her needlework to notice my tears, and maybe she had been until Sehener drew everyone's attention to me. I fixed my gaze on the floor and shook my head. I couldn't tell them. Couldn't even open my mouth because I wasn't sure what would tumble out.

"Are you nervous about tomorrow?" Merytre asked. She had been standing with Tall at the window, but now she came to sit beside Ettu. "Do you want to play a few games this afternoon? Make sure you know the rules?"

I shook my head, although that, at least, was a safe enough topic. What I had learned about Pharaoh's need to win would hardly come as a surprise to anyone in this chamber. But I feared that once I told one secret, others might tumble out.

"Play!" Tall offered. He had taken to *senet* with relish since Ahmose taught him. I supposed he had little enough to occupy his attention with.

"No," I said. "It won't matter if I don't play well."

"Lady Tiye told you to let Pharaoh win," Ettu said.

Of course it would be her who figured it out.

"She said…" My voice broke and I couldn't continue. They all waited. I kept my gaze on the floor, but I could feel their stares on me. I focused on forming the words. On not letting myself say more than I intended to. "She said it could be deadly if he didn't."

My hands clutched at my skirt as I tried to keep in my tears. I relaxed my fingers and smoothed the fabric. It was hopelessly crushed. Not that it mattered. I had no plans to leave my chambers again today and expected no visitors. Only those who lived here with me would see my wrinkled gown. And if they knew how I dreaded seeing Pharaoh tomorrow, they would think that the reason for my somber attitude. They wouldn't ask if I had learned anything else I hadn't shared with them.

"You must wear the gem from Pharaoh tomorrow," Ettu said. "But he has already seen the gown we had made to go with it and there is no time to have another made. I can't believe I didn't think of this earlier."

"I doubt he took much notice of my gown that night."

Indeed, it hadn't been until after we had eaten that he even noticed I wasn't wearing the sapphire he gifted me.

"Still," Ettu said. "You can't wear it again so soon. I really don't know what we can do."

"Come on," Merytre said, getting to her feet. "I will help you check my lady's clothing chests. There will surely be something to match that gem which Pharaoh hasn't seen her in before."

"I will help too," Sehener said, and the three of them left. I could hear them chattering on their way to my bedchamber, discussing various possibilities from my vast collection of gowns.

That left only Tall and me in the sitting chamber.

"I wish you could come with me," I said, although I regretted my words immediately on seeing how his face fell. "I'm sorry. I didn't mean to make you feel bad. I just meant I would feel safer if you were there."

I waited while he tried to find the right word to reply.

"Good!" he said at last. "Her!"

"Sehener?"

He nodded, a bashful look creeping over his face. So maybe I hadn't made him feel bad after all. Maybe he was too busy thinking about other things to pay much attention to me.

"You like her?" I asked.

He ducked his head, his mouth working, although no words came out.

"I think she likes you too," I said.

Tall made no reply, but he started flapping his hands. My words had upset him, but I wasn't sure why.

"Idiot!" he said at last.

"She doesn't think that. I have seen the two of you together. She understands you."

Better than I did. It still shamed me I hadn't listened to him as well as I prided myself. However, I couldn't change that now. All I could do was learn from my mistakes.

I could change the future for all of us. Make sure no

woman who lived in either this Palace or the other ever had reason to fear Pharaoh again. And I wasn't the only one working to achieve such an end. We might not be going about it in the same way, but at least others were doing what they could. I was not alone in my aim.

CHAPTER 38

I found myself tossing and turning that night. The babe seemed restless too, or at least I assumed it was the babe causing the odd, shivery feelings in my belly. I rested my hands over my stomach, hoping it might calm both of us.

"You don't know it yet," I whispered to him, "but you are a prince. The son of Pharaoh. You will live in a palace and have everything you could ever need. Private tutors, and servants, and lots of boys your own age to be friends with. You will never want for anything."

Saying the words out loud made me realise what an impossibly lonely life he would have. He would live in luxury, but where was his mother in all this? Who would love him? He would spend his days in Pharaoh's palace, and I would be here, confined to the Palace of the Ornaments, hoping for a rare glimpse of my son when I was invited to visit Pharaoh.

He would undoubtedly send me letters once he was old enough to compose them. Tiye said her son wrote to her every month. But how would that ever be enough for me?

How would I survive knowing my son was so close and yet a whole world away?

I gave up pretending I would fall asleep and stood at the window for a while. There were too many thoughts in my head. Too many secrets. My plan to make Pharaoh fear me. Tiye's plan to put her son on the throne. Pharaoh's murders. His need for a woman to believe she wouldn't survive. His desire to win at *senet*. Khaemmalu's kiss. Tall locked in my chambers. Half in Pharaoh's palace. How could a person hold so many secrets at once?

The cool air outside was far more inviting than lying sleepless in my bed, and before I could think it through, I changed out of my nightgown, put on a wig, and headed to the sitting chamber.

Faint lamplight indicated someone was still up and I was unsurprised to find it was Ettu. She gazed down at something small in her hand and her puffy eyes suggested she had been crying. I hesitated, wondering whether to go in or to slip back to my bedchamber. I must have made some sound, because she looked up before I could decide.

"Can't sleep?" she asked.

"I thought I would go for a walk."

"Of course." She slipped the thing in her hand into the pouch at her waist.

"What do you have there?" I asked.

She hesitated, one hand on her pouch, as if she wasn't sure she wanted to show me.

"Never mind," I said. "It's none of my business."

"No, it's all right." She took the item out and set it on her palm. "Half made it. He gave it to me before he left."

It was a wooden figurine, no taller than my thumb, with the body of a woman and a feline head. My heart stuttered a little. It's a cat, I told myself, not a lioness. But still, it was close enough to feel like one more reminder of someone trying to get a message to me.

"It's beautiful," I said. "He is very talented."

"She is Bastet. Goddess of protection. He should have taken her with him. The gods know I hardly need her protection, but he does."

Ettu tucked the little figurine away again.

"I can only hope it won't be all I have to remember him by," she said.

"I pray to Marduk he is safe, and that he returns to us soon."

She nodded, but made no reply, and I remembered her doubt about whether Marduk even existed. I wanted to ask whether she had changed her mind, but the question felt too personal. If she wanted me to know such a thing, she would tell me.

"Let's go," she said.

The hallways were quiet, with just a few runner boys and a woman I recognised as one of the kitchen staff who brought our meals each day. They all hurried past without even so much as glancing at us. Even Ettu's manly attire failed to draw their gaze. It seemed folk were becoming accustomed to seeing her dressed in such a way. It made me wonder if I could try it myself. But perhaps what was acceptable for a maid would not be tolerated on an Ornament. I wasn't sure I had the courage to try. I certainly wouldn't wear something like that to see Pharaoh. I couldn't even begin to imagine how he might react.

We made our way down the stairs and I thought I glimpsed Amankhau in the distance. If it was him, he hurried around the corner without looking back. Thank Marduk he didn't see me. I hadn't spoken with him since he tried to question me about things going missing from around the Palace. I wondered whether Panouk had told him of my accusation against him.

Neither Ettu nor I made any pretence at conversation as we reached the grounds. It was blessedly cooler out here, although there was no breeze tonight and the scent of flowers hung heavy in the air. The torches that lined the main path burned steadily and we set off in that direction. I tried not to watch for Khaemmalu. If he hid somewhere in the shadows, I would never see him unless he wanted me to, and he might avoid me after the last time we spoke. My cheeks heated as I remembered the softness of his lips against mine.

Something fluttered in my belly, although I wasn't sure whether it was nerves or the babe. We walked for some time with no sign of Khaemmalu. Eventually, we turned back and were more than halfway back to the Palace before the bushes rustled and he stepped out.

"Khaemmalu," I said, with a nod in his direction. I deliberately made my tone a little cool and restrained the smile that wanted to jump to my lips.

He bowed. "My lady."

"I have told you before you don't need to call me that," I said.

"Will you come with me?" he asked, gesturing towards the shadows. "I would speak with you in private if I may."

I hesitated. He sounded too serious to have any intention of kissing me again. Perhaps he wanted to tell me it had been a mistake. Maybe he wanted to ask if I had reported him. A glance at Ettu told me she would be of no help in my decision. She had already walked on a little further to give us the illusion of privacy. With a deep breath, I left the path and headed into the shadows. Khaemmalu followed.

Away from the light of the torches and with the moon's brilliance shielded by the trees, I could see nothing. My sandal caught on something and I stumbled, but before I could fall, Khaemmalu's hands were on my waist.

"Careful," he said. "There are exposed roots just here."

"Thank you."

I should walk on. He would let go of me once I did. But my feet wouldn't move.

His body behind me was close enough to feel his warmth. If I leaned back just the tiniest bit, my back would press against his chest. What would he do if I did that? Would his arms encircle me? Would he pull me tighter against him? Would his lips brush my neck? I shivered.

"Are you cold?" His voice was husky and right beside my ear.

"No," I breathed.

"You're trembling."

"I'm not cold."

His hands were still at my waist, burning through the thin linen of my gown. They didn't move, not even so much as a twitch of a finger.

"Kassaya," he murmured.

And suddenly, I couldn't bear it any longer. For one wild moment, I didn't care about the consequences if someone found out. His hands stayed at my waist, skimming my belly and my back as I turned.

Then I was facing him and he was no more than a few fingers' width away from me. I set my hands on his forearms, feeling his warm skin. It wasn't where I wanted to put them, but I didn't dare raise them to his chest like I longed to. His face was no more than a shadow, even as close as he was.

"There are consequences," he said.

"I know," I replied. "I don't care."

And in that moment, I truly didn't.

His lips met mine, searing me with their intensity. His hands slid around to my back. I let my hands glide up his arms until they rested on his shoulders. The muscles beneath his shirt were hard and my fingers itched to explore them. He held me firmly against his length as he kissed me in a way I had never expected to be kissed.

I'd seen kisses like this, of course. And before I met Pharaoh, I might have even hoped that one day someone would kiss me like that. When Khaemmalu finally withdrew his lips from mine, my breath caught in my throat and I was thankful for the darkness that hid my blush. I wasn't sure I could have looked him in the eyes after such a kiss.

"You should go," he whispered. "Before someone finds us."

I didn't want to let go, but he released me and stepped back. My hands fell from his shoulders and already my fingers itched to find him again.

"Good night, Kassaya," he said before he disappeared into the shadows.

CHAPTER 39

I barely slept that night, too busy reliving Khaemmalu's kiss over and over. The feel of his lips against mine, the whisper of his breath on my face, the warmth of his hands on my back as they pressed me firmly against him. But thoughts of Khaemmalu weren't the only thing on my mind. In between memories of his kiss, I reflected on Tiye's plan.

All this time, I had thought she was loyal to Pharaoh. That her entire aim was to preserve her position as his Favourite. But I had underestimated her. She was merely using her position to achieve her own aim: to place her son on the throne. It was Tiye who would be the god's mother, and never me. And she asked me to join them.

I had refused, but now I wondered whether that was the right decision. We did want the same thing, to an extent. We both wanted to see Pharaoh punished for his crimes. But she planned to elevate her son to the throne. And I had my own son to consider.

It had never occurred to me that perhaps not only Pharaoh, but also his heir, should be removed. I knew nothing about the boy, Ramses, other than what Tiye had told me, and she surely had reason to be prejudiced against him. Could he really be as unsuitable as she believed him to be? He had been raised as heir, after all. Or at least he had since Pharaoh's original heir died. He was surely trained for the duty.

Regardless of whether it was her plan or mine which came to fruition, Pharaoh would be exposed. I couldn't believe that would result in anything other than his removal from the throne. Ahmose had told me he wouldn't be imprisoned, but surely the people here wouldn't support a king who did the things he did, whether they thought him to be a god or not.

As my maids prepared me to meet Pharaoh, my mind raced between Tiye's plan and Khaemmalu. It was only Ettu clearing her throat that brought me back to the present.

"My lady, are you well?" Khensa sounded like she repeated a question already asked.

"Quite," I said.

"You seem very distracted today," Tuya said.

"Well, she is meeting with Pharaoh this afternoon," Ipu said. "I'm sure anyone would feel distracted."

I made no reply, only left them to their speculation. My gaze accidentally met Ettu's and she gave me that raised eyebrows look that told me she knew I had lied.

To my surprise, she hadn't asked any questions last night after Khaemmalu left me in the shadows. My preoccupation must have been obvious to her as we returned to my chambers, but she said not a word, which was quite unusual for her. She must have guessed what might have passed between us. I couldn't think of any other reason she wouldn't ask.

My maids dressed me in a silvery gown which draped my body in loose waves. Pharaoh's sapphire was heavy around my throat. I wished I didn't have to wear it, but he would undoubtedly notice. I didn't dare wear something else, not after the way he reacted last time. Would I have to bear this gem every time I saw him from now on? Maybe if I wore it a couple of times, he wouldn't notice if I stopped after that.

Ettu and Sehener accompanied me to the gates where my transport would be waiting. As we approached the Palace's front doors, nerves flooded through me. This was the man who killed Ishtar. Who controlled my life, even to the extent of dictating that no other man may touch me. I despised him. No, that was too mild. I hated him, even though he was the father of my babe.

I rested my hand on my belly, seeking confirmation of the child within. He was still today, blissfully unaware I was about to meet with the man who had fathered him.

If Pharaoh was so casual with the lives of his women, how did he treat his own children when there was nobody around to see? Tiye mentioned his oldest son had died. She never told me how it happened, though. Was it accident or illness? Or did he displease his powerful father in such a way that it led to his death?

I pressed my hand more firmly against my belly.

I will protect you, I promised my unborn son. *He will never harm you. No matter what I have to do, no matter the cost for me, I will keep you safe. And that starts with exposing Pharaoh.*

"My lady?" Sehener asked. "Are you ready? Your transport is probably waiting for you."

I let my hand fall from my belly as I straightened my shoulders and took a deep breath. I exhaled slowly, remembering my mother's words. *Show Pharaoh what the women of Babylon are made of.*

"Yes," I said. "I'm ready."

* * *

Kassaya's journey continues in
Book Five: *Secrets of Pharaoh*

Palace of the Ornaments Series

Book One: *Princess of Babylon*

Book Two: *Ornament of Pharaoh*

Book Three: *Child of the Alliance*

Book Four: *A Game of Senet*

Book Five: *Secrets of Pharaoh*

Book Six: *Hawk of the West*

The Amarna Age Series

Book One: *Queen of Egypt*

Book Two: *Son of the Hittites*

Book Three: *Eye of Horus*

Book Four: *Gates of Anubis*

Book Five: *Lady of the Two Lands*

Book Six: *Guardian of the Underworld*

The Amarna Princesses Series

Book One: *Outcast*

Book Two: *Catalyst*

Book Three: *Warrior*

See kyliequillinan.com for more books, including exclusive collections, and newsletter sign up.

ABOUT THE AUTHOR

Kylie writes about women who defy society's expectations. Her novels are for readers who like fantasy with a basis in history or mythology. Her interests include Dr Who, jellyfish and cocktails. She needs to get fit before the zombies come.

Swan – the epilogue to the Tales of Silver Downs series – is available exclusively to her newsletter subscribers. Sign up at kyliequillinan.com.

www.ingramcontent.com/pod-product-compliance
Lightning Source LLC
Chambersburg PA
CBHW061534210726
48287CB00006B/1949